Readers love Andrew Grey

A Taste of Love

"…an emotional story that will have you in tears one minute, smiling and laughing the next."

—Love Romances & More

A Shared Range

"…another enjoyable read filled with two well rounded and likable guys."

—Literary Nymphs

Pump Me Up

"Andrew Grey is a master storyteller. His stories have heart and the characters fairly leap off the pages to completely captivate you."

—Love Romances & More

An Unexpected Vintage

"There's nothing like a story that reminds you to get out and enjoy life!"

—Fallen Angel Reviews

Accompanied by a Waltz

"A story about first love, loss, and the rediscovery of love all wrapped up in its pages."

—Fallen Angel Reviews

http://www.dreamspinnerpress.com

Unconditional *Love*

ANDREW GREY

Dreamspinner Press

Published by
Dreamspinner Press
382 NE 191st Street #88329
Miami, FL 33179-3899, USA
http://www.dreamspinnerpress.com/

Unconditional Love

Cover Art by L.C. Chase   http://www.lcchase.com

ISBN: 978-1-61372-543-6

Printed in the United States of America
First Edition
July 2012

eBook edition available
eBook ISBN: 978-1-61372-544-3

To Sue—for introducing me to Chincoteague and inspiring the idea.

DAY 1

EARLY SUMMER
CHINCOTEAGUE ISLAND, VA

WITH a smile on his face, Donald Pottier carried the crab trap and strode across the yard toward the back door of the small house he lived in with his mother. The smile was because the trap wasn't empty, the way it had been the last few times he'd tried crabbing off the dock near his home. This time the blue crabs had been hungry for his chicken necks on a string, and he'd netted nine large ones. He and his mother would eat well.

"What did you get?" his mother asked as she opened the door, a grin breaking across her face as he held up the trap. "They're finally starting to get large enough," she commented as she took the trap and brought it into the kitchen. She handed the trap back to him before covering the kitchen table with a plastic tablecloth, and Don set the trap on it. "Don't you have to get ready for work?" she asked, pulling the large pot out from under the sink to fill it with water.

Don checked the battery-operated clock above the stove and jumped. "Yeah, if I don't move, I'm going to be late." He hurried out of the kitchen and down the hall to his small bedroom. The house his mother rented only had four rooms—living room, kitchen, and two bedrooms—but it was home and the only one Don knew. They'd lived here for as long as he could remember, renting the place from their next-door neighbor, Mrs. Klingbeil, whose house wasn't much bigger, but unlike a lot of the places in town, at least she made sure their home was maintained. He knew they were lucky, because a lot of the places on this small fishing and tourist island weren't properly taken care of by their absentee landlords.

Don opened one of the drawers in his dresser and took out a white shirt and a pair of basic black jeans. After tugging off his old jeans and T-shirt, Don pulled on the fresh clothes before checking himself in the mirror. He tried combing his wild, dark hair, but it just went right back where it wanted no matter what he did. At least the acne had started to clear up, and his face was no longer perpetually red and blotchy. His mother always said he was handsome, but Don never saw it. All he ever saw was the hair that wouldn't behave and the nose that always seemed a little crooked, even though his mother swore it was perfect.

"You're going to be late if you don't move." His mother's voice drifted in from the kitchen.

"I know, Mom. I'm almost ready to leave," Don called back, and after one more glance, he decided he looked as good as he was going to and left the bedroom. Then he joined his mother in the kitchen. "I'll see you tonight."

She hugged him before he could get away, and he decided he wasn't going to fight it. Even for a sixteen-year-old, there were worse things than being hugged by your mother. "Be careful, and call me before you leave." She released him and checked the water in the pot as the crabs struggled to get out of the trap. He hated the cooking part of the process. He would catch them, but he hated the sound of them banging on the side of the pot for the minute it took for them to die. "I'll have crab cakes for you when you get home."

"Thanks, Mom," he said with a smile, and on an impulse, he kissed her cheek before rushing out the back door to the tiny shed. He unlocked the small building and pulled out his bike. After locking the door again, he jumped on the old ten-speed and pedaling toward town.

Don kept an eye out as he rode. Sometimes cars came around the corners too fast, or he'd find one of those battery-powered carts tourists rented right in front of him. The dang things were a nuisance, but as he swerved to miss one, he kept his opinion to himself—on Chincoteague Island in the summer, the tourist was king. It was their dollars that kept the meager island economy afloat, and those tourists provided him with the job he was heading to. Reaching the main street, Don put on the brakes and checked for traffic before turning right, toward town. If he'd turned left, he could have headed across the bridges to Assateague Island with its national seashore and public beach on the ocean.

"Hey, Potty-a," a familiar, dreaded voice called from behind him, and Don pedaled faster. He was usually pretty good at avoiding Harmon Krepke and his friends, but since he'd been running late, Don had taken the most direct route, going past one of the miniature golf courses Krepke's family owned. Don could hear them behind him, and he took a quick glance as his heart rate sped up. Standing up, Don pedaled as fast as his legs would allow him, the muscles screaming even as he got closer to work. The last thing he wanted was to walk into work with dirt on his clothes again, or worse, a mouthful of stinking mud that made him gag, which had happened the last time they'd caught him.

Don could see the sign for his destination, Mr. Whippy, and he continued pedaling up the street and then turned into the parking lot. He couldn't hear the boys behind him, but he wasn't taking any chances. Coasting to a stop near the back door, he looked around and saw Harmon and his main crony, Lymon Biggs, standing near the entrance to the parking lot of the ice cream parlor, talking and laughing with each other, pointing toward him and making imaginary cutting motions across their necks. Don shivered in the almost sultry late-morning air before placing his bike with the others, making sure to lock it carefully, and then looked one last time at his taunters before going in to work.

"I thought you were going to be late," Kirsten said with her usual smile and chirpy voice as he punched his card with five minutes to spare before they opened for the day.

"I almost was," Don said, stating the obvious, but needing some time for his breathing and heart rate to return to normal. He walked to the cleaning station and filled a stainless steel bucket with water and a touch of bleach before carrying it into the dining area.

"Was Krepke chasing you again?" Kirsten asked as she took a cloth and started washing off the tables. "He's such a douche," she said sympathetically as she finished washing a table and moved on to the next. "I wish I knew what was wrong with him." Don had often wondered the same thing. He shrugged, wishing he could figure out the answer, and went outside to wipe down the plastic tables under umbrellas that lined the front of the building. He'd never done anything to him as far as he could remember, but in eighth grade, Krepke had grown faster than all the other kids. He'd started picking on most of the kids during gym class and after school, but over time his attention seemed to have focused on Don. Once Don was done with the tables, he went back inside and rinsed off his rag.

"We're opening," Mr. Hollings called as he unlocked the front doors. Their boss always made the same call, and when Don had first started working here, he'd always looked up as though a stampede of people was going to rush in. That never happened. Kirsten washed her hands and took her place behind the counter while Don finished with the tables and then joined her.

Customers began to trickle in, and by noon, there was a line. Marian, one of the other "whippers," came in, and the three of them stayed busy taking lunch orders and dipping ice cream until their fingers alternately tingled and ached from the cold.

Don rarely paid attention to the customers other than to help them and then move on to the next person, but he always noticed Jason whenever he came in. It had been an accident that he'd even learned the boy's name last summer. He and a friend had been getting cones when Don heard the friend call him about something, and Don had committed his name, as well as everything he'd ever been able to glean from his visits, to memory. Once, last year, during the hottest part of the summer, Jason had come in wearing this tank top that didn't have much to it, and Don had actually seen most of Jason's smooth chest and even his perky, pink nipples. That sight had fueled his fantasies for the rest of the summer, because Jason was beginning to look like a man instead of a boy. Don also knew that Jason and his family were summer people with a vacation house on one of the points that jutted out into the Intracoastal Waterway.

"I'd like a double scoop of Marsh Mud," Jason told him in his rich voice, and Don swallowed hard without moving for a second. Then, without saying a word, he reached for a sugar cone, because he knew that was what Jason liked, and began scooping it out for him. "I've seen you around," Jason said while Don worked the hard ice cream into a ball. "You live here on the island, don't you?"

Don placed the first scoop on the cone before making another. "Yes," he answered, a bit cautiously, even as he watched Jason lean on the case, his shirt riding up a little, and as he worked, Don could see a line of tanned skin through the glass. He nearly dropped his scoop, but managed to get the ice cream on the cone without making a complete fool of himself. Standing up, he set the cone in the stand. "Is there anything else?" Don asked, like he was supposed to.

Jason reached for the cone, taking a lick with his pink tongue, and Don used replacing his disposable gloves as an excuse to look away. "Could I get a large Coke too?"

"Sure," Don answered as he moved toward the register. He scooped some ice and then filled the cup with soda before putting a lid on it and setting it on the counter. Then he rang up the sale. "That's $4.97." Don tried not to look as Jason reached into his jeans, the fabric tightening in all the right places for a moment, and then Jason handed him a five.

"Thanks," Jason said, grabbing his soda and then walking away. Don placed the bill in the drawer and closed it, watching Jason's denim-encased rear end move as he walked toward the door. Kirsten nudged his shoulder, and he moved out of the way, turning his attention to the next customer. He knew she'd probably been trying to see where he was looking, but thankfully Jason was out of sight.

"May I help you?" he asked the next people in line, who looked like grandparents with their three grandchildren. They began telling him what they wanted, and he immediately began scooping.

Work went on like that for another hour or so. "Go ahead and take your break," Mr. Hollings told him, and Don smiled before taking off and throwing away the gloves, then heading out back. The air was warm even in the shade of the building, but it felt good, especially on his cold hands, so he leaned against the building and soaked it in.

"Do you have plans for tonight?" Kirsten asked him as she came out as well, searching her pockets for a cigarette.

"You should really stop that. You'll sound like your mother when you get older," Don teased, but he saw Kirsten nod.

"I'm cutting back to two a day," she said with a smile before lighting up. "This is my first one. Next week I'll go to one a day, and then hopefully I can stop altogether." She puffed and blew the smoke away from him. "My mom's smoked all her life, and she coughs all the time. I started because she always did it and because it was cool."

"Is it?" Don asked, and Kirsten shook her head.

"It's a bad habit. One I wished I never started, but it's hard to stop. I'm going to do it, though." She sounded determined, and Don wished her well. He never liked being around smokers much; they always smelled funny. Without thinking about it, Don snickered. The entire island smelled like dead fish, decaying marsh, and salt water everywhere you went. There was no escaping it, and he curled his nose up about a little cigarette smoke. "Don't ever start, Donny," she told him with a smirk.

Don leaned forward so he could see into the kitchen to check the clock as a multitude of muffled conversations drifted around to them from the front of the building. Don heard what sounded like a bike approach, and he tensed automatically before turning to look just as Jason pulled to a stop nearby. He watched as Jason stepped off his deep green bike that still shone with its new paint. Then, to Don's surprise, Jason walked over to where they stood. "Hey, guys," Jason said as Kirsten took another puff on her cigarette. "Taking a break from work?"

"Yeah," Don answered, wondering why Jason had stopped by and excited about it at the same time.

"How long do you work?" Jason asked, and Don's first instinct was to ask why he wanted to know, but he held back, and Jason continued. "I saw you fishing for crabs this morning, and it looked really cool. I was wondering if you'd show me how," Jason explained. "Maybe after you get off work, if you have time. I'm Jason, by the way. Jason Greene." He held out his hand like an adult, and Don stepped forward, shaking it and wondering by what twist of fate he actually got to touch the hand of the boy of his dreams.

"I'm Don Pottier, and this is Kirsten O'Connor," Don said, half expecting Jason to be using him as some sort of ruse to get to Kirsten. She turned the heads of most of the boys on the island, with her blonde hair and big chest. Not that Don really cared, but it was hard not to notice. Kirsten's mother was a ranger with the National Park Service on Assateague, and she was often referred to as Pam Anderson because she looked a lot like her, from the big blonde hair to the huge boobs. Kirsten came by her attributes honestly.

"So, are we on?" Jason asked a little earnestly.

"If you want. I'm done with work at five. We can meet here and ride to the grocery store before going back to my house, where I have a trap and other stuff we'll need," Don offered, still feeling a little reticent. But this was a chance to be with the boy who had captured his attention since the previous summer, and he might not get another.

"Cool," Jason said, "I'll meet you right here."

Don took another look in the kitchen. "We gotta get back," he said with a touch of disappointment.

"I'll meet you here at five," Jason said before hopping back on his bike and taking off, legs pumping. When Don looked away and turned to Kirsten, she had the strangest look on her face but said nothing as they walked back inside.

The rest of their shift passed in a blur of scooping ice cream, getting drinks, taking food orders, and cleaning up messes, which lasted steadily all afternoon. There were two places on the island for ice cream, and both of them were busy all day long and well into the night this time of year. In general, the employees scooped and rang up the customers. There was also always a cook to handle food orders that Don or one of the other scoopers then delivered to the tables when they were ready. They fought for those because sometimes they'd get a tip.

"What do you think of this?" Mr. Hollings asked just before the end of Don's shift, once it finally slowed down enough for them to take a two-minute breather. Their boss carried a dish with four spoons in it. This was one of the perks, or hazards of the job, depending on how you viewed it—tasting one of Mr. Hollings latest ice cream concoctions.

"What is it?" Kirsten asked as she lifted a spoon and took a bite.

"Coconut ice cream with lots of dark chocolate chips," he answered proudly. They each took a taste, and Don smiled as the flavor danced on his tongue.

"Tastes like a Mounds bar. I love those," he said. "This is great." Don smiled to reinforce his opinion. Some of Mr. Hollings's concoctions had been really bad, like the pumpkin pie he tried last fall that tasted more like stewed squash than spicy pumpkin pie. There were also the winners, like his Marsh Mud, which was a dark, heavy chocolate fudge ice cream. It was a perennial favorite—if you liked chocolate, you loved that ice cream.

"It's not really my thing," Kirsten said, "because I'm not a fan of coconut, but the flavors taste good together. I think you have a winner."

"What do you think, Marian?" Mr. Hollings asked as Marian took her first bite, and they watched her eyes widen. She was always timid about trying new flavors. Whenever she got ice cream for herself, she always got plain chocolate. "You like it?"

She nodded and grinned. "This is really good." From the look on her face, Marian had just found her new favorite flavor of ice cream, either that or there was something in there to make her

9

eyes roll into the back of her head. Mr. Hollings handed her the container with a grin of success. "You should go on your break before Don and Kirsten leave for the day."

Marian nodded, still eating the rest of the ice cream as she moved into the back room. Don couldn't help grinning as he and Kirsten took care of the last customers of their shift. Marian returned from her break, and two other people came in to relieve Don and Kirsten, so Don said goodbye to everyone before he and Kirsten left via the back door. "I'll see you tomorrow," Kirsten called as Don saw her boyfriend's car pull up, and then she hopped into the passenger seat. Through the window, he saw them kiss, and then Kirsten waved as they pulled out of the lot, waiting for traffic to clear before turning onto the main street, tires throwing up gravel.

Don watched her go and then looked around but didn't see Jason. With a sigh, he turned away from the parking lot and began unlocking his bike.

"Well, if it isn't Potty-a," Harmon Krepke said from right behind him, close enough for Don to smell his bad breath. "We're going swimming, and we thought you could cool off too."

Don stiffened and whirled around but found himself held from behind. "Leave me alone!" Don cried, trying to squirm out of Krepke's grip. But he was much bigger and stronger than Don, and he tightened his grip.

"I definitely think you need a swim. Grab his feet, Ly." Don began to kick as much as he could, but Lymon got hold of his legs and held them tight. Don kept trying to squirm, but they were too strong for him. He began to squirm even more as they carried him toward the back of the lot to where the swamp mud began. They were going to throw him in, and Don knew from firsthand experience that this wasn't just about getting dirty. There were places in the marsh that didn't have a bottom. The mud was often just thick enough that you couldn't swim in it, and yet there really wasn't a bottom you could stand on.

"Leave me alone, you jerk!" Don cried and squirmed harder as they reached the break in the fence that Mr. Hollings kept saying he needed to repair. His heart raced and his mind began to cloud as sheer panic began to sink in.

"Right here is good, now swing his legs and we'll toss him in," Krepke growled with a sinister laugh, and Don tried to see what was happening, but his head was spinning, and all he could do was try to keep struggling as both his tormenters laughed. He kept struggling and cried out as his upper body began to fall. He was caught by one arm and then the other. Opening his eyes, he realized Krepke had his arms, and he continued trying to struggle as the two bigger boys really began to swing him.

Don braced for them to let go, but then he felt his legs fall and heard shouting. "Pick on someone your own size," someone growled, and someone else cursed in pain. Lifting his head, Don saw Ly grabbing his nose, blood streaming out between his fingers. Then he was dropped, his arms released, and he fell unceremoniously onto his butt as he saw Jason turn to Krepke, fists up. Don scrambled to get out of the way as he saw Krepke brace for a punch, but Jason swept his foot in a wide arc, knocking Krepke's feet from under him. Krepke stumbled and couldn't get his balance before tumbling over the shallow bank and into the black mud. "Quit your bawling and help him out, or I'll give you some more," Jason told Ly, and the bully's eyes widened as he held his nose, blood still running down his face.

Meanwhile, Don saw Krepke begin to climb out of the marsh, covered almost to his neck in foul-smelling mud, sticks, and bits of half-decayed plants. He looked almost like some sort of marsh monster. Don stepped back and grabbed his bike. "Let's get out of here," he said, and Jason nodded. Don hopped on his bike and waited for Jason before they took off, putting as much distance as they could between them and the bullies.

Once they were on the road, Jason began to laugh.

"Aren't you afraid of getting in trouble?" Don asked Jason once they turned off the main street and they could ride side by side.

"No. Those two pick on everyone, and once word gets around that they've been whipped, someone else will do it too." Jason put on his brakes to slow down, and Don followed suit. "How often have they done stuff like that?"

"Couple of years, I guess. Usually it's just taunting and calling names," Don confessed, looking away as his face colored. He hated being afraid of them, and if he were truthful with himself, he was ashamed that he couldn't take care of himself. Every time those two got the better of him, it tore at him. What if someone tried to hurt his mother? He was the man of the family and all she had. What if he couldn't protect her when she needed it?

"So where are we going?" Jason asked, and Don smiled, grateful he'd changed the subject.

"We need to go to the grocery store and get the bait for the crabs," Don explained as he signaled and turned the corner. "Chicken necks are the best bait there is. The store stocks them cheap." Thank goodness, because Don only had a few dollars in his pocket, and he didn't want to ask Jason for money—that would hurt almost as much as being thrown in the mud. They rode into the grocery store parking lot and locked up their bikes before walking into Meatland Market. Don always had to keep himself from snickering when he thought of the name. Everyone on the island was very conservative, but they called their grocery store Meatland.

After walking through the doors, Don led the way through the aisles to the butcher counter. "Afternoon," he said to Charlie, the butcher.

"More chicken necks?" Charlie asked with a grin.

"Yup. I'm teaching Jason here how to crab. Nothing better than chicken necks." Don grinned, and Charlie began wrapping up the package.

"They're free. I was about to throw them away anyhow," Charlie said with a smile. "You say hi to your mother for me."

"I will," Don said honestly, taking the package of meat scraps. Charlie said that to him every time he came in, and Don knew it was because Charlie liked his mother. Don had always thought Charlie would be good for his mom, and he wished she wasn't alone so much, but the one time he'd mentioned it to his mother, she'd gotten testy, with that "I'm your mother" look in her eye that Don knew better than to argue with. Saying goodbye, they walked through the checkout and showed the package to the cashier before hurrying to their bikes. Don fastened the package to the carrier on the back of his using a bungee cord, and then they were off.

The ride to Don's house took about ten minutes. Don walked his bike to the shed and put it away after showing Jason where he could put his. "I'm always pretty careful." He was always afraid Krepke would come by and damage his one mode of transportation other than his feet, so he kept his bike locked away when he could.

"Who's your friend?" Don's mother called from the back door, and he hurried up the steps. Like most of the houses on the island, theirs was on stilts to protect it from storm surges. At its highest point, the island stayed above water during a major storm, but that was just the areas near the main part of town. The rest of the island often submerged under storm conditions.

"This is Jason," Don said, and Jason shook hands with his mother.

"It's very nice to meet you, Mrs. Pottier. Don is going to show me how to catch crabs." Jason actually said that, and Don bit his lower lip to keep from snickering.

"Dinner is ready, so why don't you two come in and eat? You can fish afterwards," his mother said before stepping back from the door. "Do you need to call your mother to let her know where you are?" Jason looked at his watch and shrugged. "Call her, and then come eat." His mother pointed toward the phone, and Jason dialed the number, but it sounded like he just left a message.

Don took Jason to wash up, and as he passed through the house, he saw it through Jason's eyes, and he felt himself coloring. The furniture was old and worn around the edges. Nothing matched, and it all seemed shabby. But it was what they had and could afford. "Your mom's really nice," Jason said with a shoulder bump as they washed up and headed back to the kitchen.

"I made the crab cakes with what Don caught this morning," his mother explained, placing a plate in front of each of them. Don noticed that his mother didn't join them right away, and it wasn't until Don asked her that she finally filled a plate and sat at the table. It didn't take a scientist to figure out that there wasn't much food and she was going to do without. Don peered at Jason, thinking he might have seen it too. Part of Don was as embarrassed as sin, but when Jason didn't say anything, he felt better.

"These crab cakes are amazing, Mrs. Pottier," Jason said with a grin. "I've had them in the restaurants on the island, but they don't hold a candle to these." His mother smiled, and Don saw her soak in the praise. The embarrassment that had

14

threatened to well up slipped away when he realized that Jason might have understood.

Once they were done eating, Don took the plates to the sink and rinsed them, not that there was much left. "Just stack them in the sink and see if you can catch a few more crabs," she told them.

"Thanks, Mom," Don said, and he led Jason toward the door.

"Thank you for a great meal, Mrs. Pottier," Jason said before following him outside.

Don got the package of necks along with the heavy string, net, and cage. "Let's go. I usually crab at Mr. Winters's place." Don pointed toward the end of one of the channels. "You need access to the salt water." Don began walking, and Jason strode next to him, after a while taking the cage.

"What's this for?" Jason asked, holding it up.

"The crabs need to be kept alive until you cook them, so we'll put the ones we catch in there and keep it in the water so they stay alive. When we get back, Mom will steam them right away and then we can eat them. Mom has this secret set of spices that she uses when she cooks them." Don grinned as they walked. "I've eaten these crabs for almost my whole life, and no one makes them better than my mom."

"I believe that," Jason said softly as they continued walking. "Have you always lived here on the island?"

"Yes. My mother was raised here and so was my dad. He was a fisherman. He had his own boat, and one day he went out and never returned. I was about five, and I remember my mother worrying and crying for days before she told me that my dad wasn't coming back." Don swallowed hard. "I barely remember him now, except that he was the one who taught me how to go crabbing. I don't have many memories of my dad, but I can remember when he took me in the car to what must have been a friend's dock, and he tied the chicken necks on the strings and set them in the water. Then we waited, and I remember how he played with me and then showed me how to test the lines." Don tried to remember his father's face, but he couldn't. He'd been too young, and all he could remember was how happy he'd felt with his dad.

They walked along one of the roads farther from town. Most of the homes were relatively new vacation places. "How far is it?" Jason asked.

"Next house on the right," Don answered, and then motioned for them to cut through the yard. Don waved to Mr. Winters, who sat in the shade on his deck, and he waved back.

"Twice in one day," Mr. Winters called down.

"Just showing my friend how to do it," Don said, and Mr. Winters waved one more time and settled back in his chair as they continued on to the channel wall. "This is perfect because it isn't too deep and the channel goes out to the ocean. The crabs love it here because there's lots of food and the water isn't too rough." Don set down the supplies, and Jason placed the cage on the dock.

"What do we do?" Jason asked, and Don handed him the ball of string.

"Cut off two pieces about yay long"—he motioned with his hands—"and I'll show you how to tie on the bait. If you don't do it right, the crabs will steal it." Don opened the package of meat, taking a few minutes to show Jason how he had to tie them on. "Now tie a loop in the other end," he said, demonstrating, "and lower it into the water. Put the loop over the hooks, and now we wait." Don sat on the dock, becoming quiet, the way he usually was when he was out here. Crabbing was usually his chance to think, and he fell into that mode without really trying.

"Do you know what happened to your dad?" Jason asked after a few minutes. "I mean, did you ever find out?"

Don shook his head slowly. "The coast guard believes he sank in a storm off the coast, but we never knew for sure. There was what they believed was a distress call, but then nothing. The coast guard figured he went down fast." Don tested each of the strings, but there was nothing there. "For a long time," Don said as he shifted so he was facing Jason, "I used to dream that somehow he escaped and that he would show up. I suppose that for both Mom and me there's a part of us that still hopes, even though we both know he isn't going to come back. I think that's why she won't get serious about anybody."

"Does your mom date much?"

Don shook his head again. "A few times, but I know she still hasn't let go of my dad." Don checked the lines again and felt the familiar extra weight and tug. "Grab the net," he told Jason, "and lift the string. Don't pull it out of the water or the crab will let go. Once you can see it, scoop it up from underneath." Don watched Jason's excitement when he saw the crab just below the surface. He scooped the net and came up with both the chicken neck and the crab. "Perfect!" Don cried and motioned for Jason to lower it onto the dock. "Unfortunately, it's not big enough." Don used his fingers to show how large they needed to be. "You need to catch it by the back and lift it out of the net," Don explained, and he demonstrated what he'd done half a million times. Once the small crab was free, Don walked down a ways and dropped it back into the water.

"Why let it go down there?" Jason asked.

"If I didn't, we'd just catch it again. Now put it back in the water and feel the other lines." Don sat on the dock again and watched as Jason slowly lifted the other lines to see if they had anything. "Scoop it up," Don encouraged, and Jason got the crab that was there. This time it was a big one, and Don worked it out of the net before placing it into the cage. After making sure the door was secure, he lowered the cage into the water, tying the rope around one of the pilings. "You just caught your first crab. You're a fisherman now," Don told Jason, and he seemed inordinately pleased. "So where do you live when you aren't on the island?"

"Chicago," Jason answered. "My mother grew up outside DC, and she remembered coming here when she was a kid, so a few years ago, she and Dad bought the place here because they thought it would be a great place to spend the summers."

Don listened as Jason talked. He could hardly believe that they were sitting like this talking. Part of him expected Jason to get up at any second, tell him that his crabs and chicken necks tied to strings were stupid, and storm away. But he didn't. He kept talking, and Don listened intently as he watched each movement of Jason's body. Part of him wondered what someone like Jason could possibly see in him, but they both seemed to be having fun, so he decided not to worry about it.

"Are both your parents here now?" Don asked when he realized Jason had been talking and he wasn't really listening.

"No. My dad is in Chicago working, and I think my mother is in DC," Jason said matter-of-factly, and Don gasped before they both looked up at Mr. Winters's deck, but it was empty.

"You mean they're both gone and you're here alone?" Don couldn't believe it.

"She'll be back in a day or so. It's no big deal. I spend most of the school year away when I'm at school. She doesn't stay away for very long." Jason turned away, checking the lines and netting another crab. Don watched Jason as he removed the crab

18

from the net. He was being really careful to avoid the claws, and it took him a while, but he got it out and into the cage. Don checked the doors before they lowered it back into the water. As they worked, Don couldn't help wondering what Jason's life must be like. He obviously had all kinds of *things,* judging by the clothes and the new bike, but his parents had left him alone on the island. It made Don feel lucky, and that was something he'd rarely felt in his life. He had his mother, and while they might not have had much in stuff, Don knew he was loved. His mother would never think of leaving him alone for days at a time. His mother worked two jobs and always managed to see to it that she was there for important events, and she always had dinner for him. Sometimes she wasn't around a lot because of her schedule, but she was always there for him.

"Must be lonely. Do you have friends on the island?"

"One," Jason said with a smile, and Don felt himself blush when he realized Jason was talking about him. "I met a kid last summer, but his family was only renting a place, and they were gone after a week." Jason fiddled with a small pile of sand that had accumulated on the boards.

"It must get lonely being by yourself all the time," Don said, knowing he was probably stating the obvious. "I spend a lot of time alone myself. Mom works a lot, and when I'm not scooping ice cream, I'm usually crabbing, fishing, or hunting for oysters." Don absently checked the lines, but there was nothing. "It's what I can do to help."

"What do you want to do?" Jason asked, and Don looked at his new friend a little confused.

"Do? About what?" Don thought Jason might have been getting bored and prepared to get everything together.

"When you get older. What do you want to be?"

Don shrugged. "I haven't thought about it much. There isn't much to do on the island. I never gave it much thought. Mom says I have to finish high school, and then after that I figured I'd start working on one of the boats." There wasn't much else he could do to earn a living. "I know I can't scoop ice cream forever."

"Don't you want to go to college?" Jason asked, standing up as one of the lines moved. "I bet you get good grades." Jason pulled it up and scooped the crab, but it was too small, so he let it go. "My folks would kill me if I didn't go on to college. I get pretty good grades, and I work hard, but I don't know what I want to do either. My dad wants me to become a doctor like him. He's a plastic surgeon and makes a fortune giving women boob jobs and butt lifts." Jason rolled his eyes.

"I never got what the big deal was about," Don said, and then he wanted to suck the words back in. He really hadn't understood boobs because they held no interest for him, but that statement was probably a little more telling than he'd intended or was good for him. Don checked the strings again and then got the net, scooping up another small crab that he carried down the way and released, silently berating himself the entire time for his big mouth. Walking back, Don kept his head down as he sat on the dock, trying to figure out a way to cover his mistake.

"I don't get it either," Jason said after a long time, and Don saw him lift his eyes. Was Jason saying what he thought he was saying? His heart raced, and he suddenly got all weird-feeling in his stomach, like he was both scared and excited at the same time. Looking up, he met Jason's gaze and he saw the same longing and fear reflected back at him.

"Hey, boys," Mr. Winters called from the deck above them. "You should probably call it a night."

Don checked his watch. They'd been crabbing and talking for about an hour. The sun was starting to go down. Don pulled in the lines and cut loose the chicken, throwing it into the water. "The crabs will eat it and get bigger." Then he pulled out the cage and looked at the two crabs inside. "We should probably release them. There aren't enough to do anything with."

Jason looked a little disappointed. "I guess so," he agreed, and Don opened the door, setting the cage in the water, and the crabs skittered out and away. Then they gathered all their things, including the papers, throwing them in Mr. Winters's trash before heading out toward the road. "Thank you," Don called up to the deck, but he didn't hear an answer.

"We could walk down to my place," Jason offered. "It's toward the end of this road."

Don looked up at the sky. It was still light, but it would be dark in an hour or so. "I can't stay very long. Mom will worry if I'm out after dark."

"I don't think it's very far," Jason said, and they walked down the side of the road, passing a number of nice summer places on stilts. As they walked, the houses seemed to get nicer and somewhat larger. Don saw the end of the road, and Jason veered off to the right and down a drive that opened up to a large lot with a tall, white beach house on painted stilts. The place was huge, and Don was about to ask if this was the place when Jason began to climb the wide, almost grand-looking steps to the door.

Don set the net and cage under the steps and walked up after Jason. He knew no one was home, but there was a nice car parked in a neatly manicured parking spot. Reaching the top of the steps, Don saw Jason pull out a key and unlock the door. "Come on," Jason said, and he opened the door, motioning for him to go inside.

Don stepped in and it seemed like he'd walked into another world. That entire floor looked like one huge room, with glistening, sand-colored floors and a kitchen with gleaming white cabinets and countertops in what looked like deep-brown mottled stone. Everything about the place screamed a lot of money, including the large television in the corner. Don had never seen one that big except in the sports bar in town, and somehow he doubted that one was this big. "I have Nintendo, if you'd like to play," Jason offered, and Don nodded slowly, feeling like a fish out of water.

"I played once at a cousin's birthday party," Don admitted, and he saw Jason's mouth fall open, but he didn't comment.

Jason set up the system. "I don't have any of the really cool games here—they're at home with the newer one."

Don did a double take. "You have two?" Don could only wish he had video games, but to have two of them boggled his mind. "You're really lucky."

Jason shrugged. "My dad bought me one for my last birthday because he forgot he'd gotten me one the year before. Or, I should say, my dad's assistant bought it for me." Jason started the game and then demonstrated how to play. Then he let Don play. He didn't do very well, and his Mario guy ended up dying really fast, but Jason let him play again, and he did better with Jason coaching him. After playing a few times, he handed the controller back, and Jason played for a while, getting really far in the game. They took turns playing, shouting at each other's success.

"I should get home. It's getting dark," Don said, looking out the windows.

"Call your mom and see if you can stay a while longer," Jason asked with this adorable "don't leave me all alone" look on his face, and Don felt himself cave immediately. He found the phone in the kitchen and checked the time before dialing the number. His mother picked up on the first ring.

"Where are you? I was getting worried."

"I'm at Jason's. He has cool video games. I'm going to stay a little longer, and then I'll come home."

His mother didn't say anything at first. "Be home in an hour," she said, and Don thanked her before hanging up. When he returned to the living room area, Jason flipped him the controller, and Don began a game. It went on for what seemed like forever. It was one of those moments when everything seemed to come together and whatever he did was right. Don's brain flashed ahead in the game, almost able to predict what it would do before it happened.

"Sweet," he heard Jason say from behind him as he advanced a level, the action moving faster as mushrooms came at him from almost all directions. With a jump, he leapt over the group, bounding off the tops of them to reach the plateau. Then he wasn't quite sure what to do, and the game ended. "Dude," Jason said from behind him. "That was awesome. You got to areas I've never seen. That was way cool."

Don put down the controller, his entire body singing with video game excitement. When he turned, he saw Jason smiling at him, and their eyes locked like they had on the dock. Neither of them moved, and Jason's tongue licked his plump lips.

"Don, I saw you watching me today at Mr. Whippy, and I liked it." Don's throat closed and suddenly he couldn't breathe. "It was nice," Jason said, and Don's mind began to process what he was hearing. "I don't get girls, either, and they don't do anything for me." Don knew his words were going to come back to haunt him.

"Are you...." Don wanted to ask, but he couldn't bring himself to say the word. He'd heard it way too many times used to cut at people as the ultimate insult.

"Gay?" Jason supplied, and Don nodded. Jason didn't answer, and instead Don saw him moving closer. Then their lips met, and Don wasn't quite sure what to do, but he was kissing Jason, or Jason was kissing him. Not that it mattered, because they were kissing and he liked it. Jason moved back, and Don flicked his tongue over his lips so he could get another taste of Jason. Then Jason kissed him again, and this time Don definitely kissed back.

It felt like electric shocks went all up and down his body. He could barely think, and his lungs were running out of air, but the last thing he wanted to do was stop for something as stupid as breathing. When they pulled apart, Don heard them both gasp for breath. "I have to go home," Don said softly, not wanting to leave at all, but his mother would be angry if he didn't leave right away.

Jason nodded in the light of the television. "Do you have to work tomorrow?"

"No. I was going to go fishing, though," Don said.

"We could go to the beach if you want," Jason offered, and Don smiled.

"The best fishing places are on Assateague. We could fish and swim," Don explained, and Jason grinned before hurrying to the counter to write something down. "Here's the number here. Why don't you call me in the morning, and I can pick up my bike?"

"Okay," Don agreed, and Jason gave him another quick kiss. Then Don said goodbye and hurried down the steps. He grabbed the net, cage, and his ball of string before looking up to see Jason standing outside the door. He waved and then took off

24

at a run down the dimly lit street, trying to get home before his mother killed him. He had a ways to go, and unlike during the day, he had to stick to the streets because he couldn't see. By the time he reached home, it was full-on night, and he put Jason's bike and his other things away in the shed, making sure to lock it before walking into the house. His mother hadn't come out to either greet or scold him, which was unusual, and he found her in the living room asleep in a chair. "I'm home, Mom," he said quietly, and she came awake. Don kissed her on the cheek. "I'm going to go to bed."

"Did you have a good time?"

Don tried not to blush, because he'd had the best time he could possibly imagine. "Yeah. We caught a few crabs but let them go. We talked a lot and played video games at his house. He's really cool."

"That's good, honey," his mother said with a yawn. "I'm awfully tired, so I'm going to go to bed." Don glanced at the clock. It was just after ten, and his mother never went to bed without watching the evening news.

"Are you feeling okay?" he asked when he noticed that she seemed to be walking a little funny.

"I'm fine. Just a little tired, and I have to get up to work at the store tomorrow." She smiled and gave him a good-night hug before going into her room and closing the door. Don locked up the house and turned off the lights before showering quickly and then brushing his teeth. After slipping on a pair of briefs, he climbed into bed and lay awake, staring at the ceiling with a grin on his face. And all he could think about was that he'd gotten his first kiss from a boy—Jason, his new friend.

Don had been pretty well convinced that he was the only person who felt the way he did. Everyone at school acted like being gay was the worst possible thing in the world, and all he had ever heard about were limp-wristed guys who talked with lisps and acted like girls. But Jason was cool, smart, and he'd beaten both Ly and Harmon, sending the bully into the marsh. That was something he'd relish for the rest of his life, as was the feel of Jason's lips when he'd kissed him. The memory was enough to send a tingle up his spine and to get him majorly excited. Don was about to do something about that when he heard his mother coughing in the next room. She'd been doing that sometimes—she'd go on for a while and then stop.

Getting out of bed, he made sure he wasn't sporting wood before leaving his room and knocking on his mother's door. "Are you okay?" He opened it and peered inside, and he saw his mother doubled up on the bed. "Do you want some water?" She nodded, and Don hurried to the sink, bringing her back a glass of water. She took a sip and then another before settling back on the bed.

"I'm okay, Donny, thank you," she said, and he set the glass on the bedside table before leaving the room and going back to his own. Getting in bed, he kept listening for more coughing. But he heard none, and then his adolescent mind returned to the memory of his first kiss and the fact that tomorrow he was going to get to see Jason in a bathing suit.

DAY 2

NEARLY A YEAR LATER
CHINCOTEAGUE ISLAND, VA

THE phone rang, and Don rushed for it so the noise didn't wake his mother. "Jason, that better be you," he said and heard a deep laugh come through the phone. "So do you want to go to the beach? I have the day off, and it looked like it should be really nice."

"You bet," Jason answered, his voice lowering. "I've wanted to see you in a bathing suit since we got here last week, but all it's done is rain. If it's okay, I'll come by in an hour and pick you up. Maybe we can do something fun in town before heading to the beach."

"Great, I'll see you then. I have something I'd like to show you when you get here." Don hung up and heard his mother stirring in her room. Then she came out, already dressed. "Did the phone wake you?" Don asked, and she shook her head.

"I was up already," she said, and Don saw how nicely she was dressed, which she noticed as well. "I have an appointment after my shift at the restaurant, so I'll head right into work at the store after." One of his mother's jobs was part-time cashier at the Family Dollar store on the far side of the island, near the bridge to Assateague Island. Stuff there was cheap, and she got a discount, so a lot of the things they needed came from there, including most of his clothes. The stuff at the tourist shops was nicer but a lot more expensive. "I'll see you tonight," she said quietly. There was something in her tone that worried him. "You have a fun day off, and I'll see you when I get out of work." She left the house, and a few minutes later, he heard his mother's old car pull away.

Alone in the house, Don finished getting dressed before sitting down at the desk in the corner of his room and starting his computer. He wanted to get everything ready before Jason got here. He'd been working through a problem since before Jason got there for the summer, and last night he'd finally fixed it, so it was time to show his baby to somebody. And that somebody had to be Jason. As he finished getting everything set, he heard a car pull up and then a knock on the door.

"Jay, is that you? Come on in," Don called, and he heard the door open and close. He'd begun using the nickname in their e-mails over the winter. Turning from the screen, Don looked toward the door and saw Jay standing in the doorway. His breath hitched, and without thinking, he stood up. Don took a step closer, and Jay crashed into him, their lips connecting in a deep kiss. Between the end of last summer, when Jason had left with his family, and seeing him again this summer, Don knew he'd fallen in love with the other boy. So far they'd only kissed and touched, sometimes pretty intensely, but last summer things had been so tentative. Today, as soon as Don saw Jay again, his heart had bloomed and it seemed like the world had opened up for him.

They broke the kiss at the same time, grinning like Cheshire cats. "So what was it you wanted to show me?" Jay asked, and Don blinked a few times to clear his mind, trying to remember.

"Oh, yeah," he said, and Jay laughed before kissing him again.

"I love that I can make you forget everything," Jay told him once he pulled his lips away. "Now show me what's got you so excited besides me."

Don laughed and moved toward the computer. "Do you remember how last summer we played video games until our hands hurt?'

"Tell me about it. You got so you beat me at almost everything," Jay fake groused before bursting into a smile.

"Well, I've been working on my own video game," Don said. "I based it on the things we do here." He started the game. "I call it *Catching Crabs*. You have to procure your bait and then use it to catch the crabs." The game started and Don moved through it, showing Jay the various levels. Jay was quiet as Don looked at the screen. "As you go on, the crabs get smarter, and the bigger they are, the harder they are to catch. I also made the net smaller and smaller in each round, and certain crabs have the ability to open the cage if you don't fasten their claws."

"This is freakin' awesome!" Jay cried, and Don couldn't stop a grin. "How did you do all this?"

"I found some of the graphic software at one of the stores in town, and when we made our Christmas shopping trip to Annapolis, I asked my mom for an animation program. Then I put it all together."

"You're a genius, you know that?" Jay hugged him from behind, and Don felt his friend's chin rest on his shoulder. "It's amazing what you've been able to do."

"I couldn't have done it without you, ya know."

"How so? All I did was show you how to play video games," Jay said.

"You're the one who gave me the computer, remember?" Don said. At the end of the previous summer, Jason had said that they should keep in touch. He'd told Don that his dad was getting him a new laptop computer for school, so Jay had presented Don with his old computer. "You told me your dad didn't even remember that he'd given you a computer two years before, so you passed it on to me. I could never have done any of this without you." Don stopped talking because what he was about to say next was too girly for words. Developing the game had helped him feel closer to Jay.

"It was purely selfish on my part. I gave it to you so we could e-mail each other, and instead you created this wonderful world. I love it." Jay leaned closer, and Don could smell Jay's clean, earthy scent. "Have you given any more thought to college? You have so much talent. I use a computer all the time, but you created something unique with it."

"I have, but there's no way we can afford it," Don explained. He wasn't lying. He'd talked to counselors and looked into schools he could attend, but even with financial aid, there would still be thousands of dollars that he would have to come up with that he would never be able to find. "Maybe after I've had a chance to save some money I can go in a few years." He really didn't want to talk about this now, or ever, for that matter. Don didn't envy Jay much. His family might have money, but Don knew he had what really mattered, which was family who loved him. Still, it was times like this, when he wanted something so badly and the doors were closed to him, not because of his talent or grades, but because of money, that he wished he could trade places with Jay. Don felt Jay lightly pat his shoulder.

"How about we head downtown and have some fun. Grab a bag for the beach, and we'll get going. But you have to promise me you'll give me a chance at this game later. I really want to play it," Jay said, and Don nodded and began packing his things for the beach. He didn't say much as he packed, his thoughts momentarily on what he knew he couldn't have. "I'm sorry, Donny, I shouldn't have brought it up."

Don held his breath a minute. "It's not your fault," he said softly, wondering how he could tell Jay that it was all his fault. Jay, just by being his friend, had shown him and told him about so many things that Don wanted them and wanted to see them, but he knew that wasn't in the cards. That computer Jay had given him had opened up a world he hadn't known existed a year ago, and now he wanted more, but it was closed to him, and he knew it. Throwing the last of his things in the bag, Don set it on the bed and put his wants aside with a deep sigh. Nothing was going to change today, and he wanted to enjoy his day off, so he smiled and tried to forget about it for now.

"Do you know what I'm in the mood for?" Jay asked with one of his patented grins, guaranteed to mean trouble. "Pirate miniature golf."

"You want to get me killed next year in school, don't you?" Don said with a grin.

"Has Krepke still been bothering you?" Jay asked, his eyes becoming hard.

"Not really. He basically leaves me alone now," Don answered, but he didn't tell Jay that was because he had younger kids to pick on now. The guy was a menace.

"Then let's go play some golf. And I brought my camera, so we can get a good picture of Pirate Harmon." Jay began singing some obscene version of a sea chantey as he walked through the house, and Don followed, shaking his head a few times before laughing his ass off.

Don put his bag in the trunk of Jay's new car and slid into the passenger seat. "This is really nice," Don said, running his hand over the upholstery, knowing that Jay's dad had bought it for him. When he'd first seen Jay that summer, Don wasn't surprised that he had a new car as much as the fact that it was an Escort as opposed to some sort of sports car. Jay seemed thrilled with it and insisted on taking Don anywhere he wanted to go. The car Don's mother had always seemed to be on the verge of expiration, but somehow the old thing kept going. Jay started the engine and backed out of the driveway before heading toward town.

It was a glorious day, and Don's mood improved very quickly as they rode with the windows down, Bon Jovi blasting on the radio, and when Jay's hand slid into his, the last of his frustration melted away and everything felt right. The sun shone, and Jay opened the console, grabbing a pair of sunglasses that he slid on, then he handed Don an identical pair. Don's joy lasted until they pulled into Pirate Cove Adventure Golf. Don had to admit this was the best miniature golf course in town, with waterfalls and greens that moved, but once they'd parked, the first person Don saw was Harmon Krepke glaring at him. Don knew that the only reason Jay came here was so he could "poke the bear." "This place is great, and I won't let Harpoon Harmon ruin our fun," Jay said. He turned toward the entrance booth and smiled at Krepke sitting in it, dressed as a pirate in a huge hat. He should have looked silly, but even in that getup, Krepke managed to look mean.

"Two," Jay told him after striding up to the booth, holding a twenty.

"Your money isn't any good here," Harmon ground out between his teeth. Don felt uncomfortable and just wanted to leave, but Jay looked around him and saw two carloads of people pull in and open their car doors.

"You're closed?" Jay said loudly. "That's too bad. We'll just have to go down the street." Car doors closed behind them, and Don peeked and saw the cars pulling away. "I can do that all day," Jay said, staring at Harmon, who looked about ready to jump over the counter any second.

"What's all this?" A man came up beside them, an older version of Harmon. "We're definitely open." He glared at his son before turning to them, ringing up Jay's purchase, and handing them clubs and golf balls. "Have fun," he told them, and as they walked through the entrance, Don heard what he thought was a smack. Looking back, he saw Harmon's hat was askew and he was rubbing the side of his face. For a second, he felt sorry for Harmon, seeing the hurt expression of a kid who simply wanted his father's approval and couldn't seem to get it, but then Harmon saw Don looking and the usual sneer fell into place. Don turned away, following Jay to the beginning of the course.

He had more fun than he'd had since Jay left last year. It was early enough in the day that the real heat hadn't had a chance to build, and the breeze felt wonderful. When they got to the second set of nine holes, Jay stopped. "Loser buys lunch," he said before teeing off. Jay easily won the first hole, and Don the next. They tied many of them, but on the second to the last one, Don flubbed it and ended up needing five strokes. While Jay teed off at the last hole, Don mentally counted the amount of money in his pocket because he knew he was going to lose. Jay shot close to the hole and Don lined up his shot and hit it even closer, the ball stopping on the edge of the cup before slowly tipping in. Don jumped and hooted at his hole in one, but he knew he was still going to lose as Jay easily tipped his ball into the cup. Jay marked the scores and handed Don the card.

"Looks like you win," Jay said with a huge smile followed by a pat on the back. "We'll have winner's lunch at the Starfish before we head out to the beach," Jay told him before taking the clubs and handing them in.

Don looked down at the card and saw that he had indeed won, but as he looked over the scores for the holes, he saw where

Jay had added a stroke to his own score or shaved off the stroke from Don's. He looked at Jay, who was talking and laughing with the kid behind the counter, and Don silently slid the card into his pocket and joined him.

Back in the car, Jay drove to the Starfish sandwich stand, and once they had their food, Jay put the sandwiches in the cooler in the trunk, along with their drinks, and drove across the island. Kirsten's mother greeted them at the entrance to the national seashore, waving them through, and they drove down to the beach. Jay parked, and they carried their things down to the shore and spread an old blanket and their towels on the sand. Don pulled off his shirt and was about to grab his bag when he saw Jay do the same thing. It had been a year since he'd seen Jay like this, and, man, had he changed. The hints of a boy's body that had still been present a year ago had been replaced by the attributes of a strong young man. He wasn't bulky, but Don knew Jay could be if he wanted to. Instead, he was lean, with a tiny waist and wide shoulders. Don tried not to be too obvious because there were a lot of people around, but he couldn't take his eyes off Jay for a second.

"Don, are you going to change?"

He nodded, his mouth too dry to talk. He saw Jay smile, and then Don picked up his bag and hurried to the changing rooms. When he returned, Jay was lying on his stomach in the sun, and Don took a minute to admire his wide shoulders. He fully intended to admire the rest of him, but his eyes stopped at a tattoo on Jay's shoulder. "What's that?"

"I got it this winter. Do you like it?" Jay said, lifting his head to wink at Don. The design wasn't large and was made of what appeared to be almost curling vines, but as Don looked he could see that the vines made definite shapes. "Do you see it?" Jay asked, lowering his head again, and Don kept looking. Slowly two things appeared out of the perceived randomness: a D and a

P. Jay had had Don's initials tattooed on his shoulder. Don didn't know what to say. He sort of fumbled for words and ended up flopping down on his towel.

"Why did you do that?" Don asked.

"Because now you'll be with me forever," Jay answered softly, but he didn't say anything more, and Don watched as Jay's eyes closed.

"I have some suntan lotion in my bag," Don said, reaching for it, and he sat up and began to smooth it into his skin. He didn't get sunburned too much, but as strong as the sun was, he didn't want to end up in pain. After handing the bottle to Jay, he began smoothing some on, and they passed the bottle back and forth. Once they'd gotten everywhere they could reach themselves, Jay smoothed some onto Don's back for him. Don then took the bottle and squirted some lotion into his hands. Jay turned around, and Don used the lotion as a cover to run his hands up and down Jay's back and sides, sun-warmed skin passing under his hands as waves crashed, the wind blew, children laughed, and sea birds called to one another overhead.

Don closed the top of the lotion bottle and lay on his towel next to Jay, listening to the sounds all around him but hyperaware of whatever Jay did, from his breathing to that little twitch in his foot that he did sometimes. Eventually his mind settled, and Don closed his eyes, letting the warmth carry him away.

Cool water dripping onto his back made him start, and he sat up, ready to either run or fight, but Jay just grinned at him as his suit dripped. "The water's great, Donny," Jay said with a grin. "Come on in." Jay raced back into the surf, and Don stood up before following him in. The water was cool, and it always took Don a few minutes to get used to it. However, this time he'd just gotten up to his waist when he was bowled over and carried under by one of Jay's flying leaps. When he came up, Jay was laughing, and Don launched himself at him. Soon the play became an excuse to touch. Jay would laugh and joke even as his hands stroked Don's belly under the water. His hands felt so good that a few times Don had to stifle a moan, especially when he felt Jay's hand skim just above the waistband of his suit.

"Jay," Don murmured softly, and then Jay slid his hand into his suit. Don was in heaven and couldn't believe the difference between the feel of Jay's hand on him and his own. He wanted to float and beg Jay to touch him like this forever, but some other kids got close in their play, and Jay slipped his hand out before he began swimming away. Don stood with his feet resting on the sandy bottom, watching as Jay bobbed on the waves with a huge grin on his face. Don waited for his dick to stop tenting his suit before getting out of the water. Dripping onto the sand, Don watched Jay show his body-surfing prowess for a few minutes before opening the cooler and pulling out a can of root beer.

Don sipped from the soda as Jay joined him, flopping down on his towel before grabbing his sandwich and handing Don the other one. Don wanted to ask Jay what was going on. Up to now, they'd kissed a lot and touched, but last summer they were too shy to go beyond that. Things seemed to have changed for Jay now, and not that Don was complaining, but he had so many questions, and he wasn't sure how to ask them. "That mind of yours is going a mile a minute, isn't it?" Jay said as he took a huge bite, and Don nodded, using the sandwich to cover some of his own insecurities. He felt ready for more with Jay, but what if Jay didn't like him once he saw him naked? What if he did something wrong?

Don took another bite and shook his head, trying to banish the teenage girl that appeared to have taken over his brain. "I know I'm being stupid," Don said, and Jay put his sandwich down on the paper.

"There's nothing stupid about the way you feel, and there's nothing wrong with it, either. Last year in school, three of the boys came out of the closet, and two of them went to one of the dances together. Everyone thought the prefect was going to have a cow, but they did it, and they danced together and everything."

"What happened to them?" Don knew Jay went to an expensive private school with all kinds of rules and honor codes.

"Nothing. The dean tried to initiate proceedings for expulsion, but they actually used the honor code against him because they were being true to themselves and honest about who they were. It was sort of eye-opening for everyone." Jay opened a soda and took a sip before setting it on the sand. "My dad had a shit fit, though, and threatened to pull me out of school." Jay's smile faded away. "I always thought of my dad as being pretty easygoing and open-minded, but I guess that's a show, like everything else." Jay sighed, and Don tried to think of a time when he'd seen Jay like this and couldn't. "I never saw it before, but everything in my family is about how things look. My dad drives a really expensive car, and my mom has one that's almost identical. We have a big house outside Chicago and the place here. My dad works constantly, probably to pay for it all and my mother's shopping trips. They're just so shallow, and neither of them has any idea who I really am. My mother left three days ago. She's outside DC at some spa getting mud baths and God knows what else, my dad is in Chicago, and I'm here alone."

"It's okay, Jay. I'm here with you," Don said, not knowing what else to say.

"I know," Jay said, and then he quieted. They ate the rest of their lunches without saying anything. When they were done, Don wadded up the trash and placed it in the cooler. "You know what really sucks? I get top grades in school, and I'll probably be at the top of my class when I graduate in a year. Best student in the whole fucking school, and the only time my dad gives a fisherman's fuck about anything is when some of the guys at school come out because they're gay." Jay pulled his knees to his chest, resting his head on them. "The one time I want him to stay away and let things be is the time he gets involved." Jay began absently digging in the sand in front of him. "My folks don't have a clue who I am, and what's worse, they don't give a damn."

"I'm sure that's not true," Don said, mainly because it was hard for him to imagine his mother not caring about him. He'd always known that his mom was the one thing he had going for him over Jay, and it was probably the one thing Jay envied about him.

"I know it is, Donny. They buy me things so they can brush me aside. Half the time they don't even know what they're buying." Jay continued digging, making the hole in the sand bigger. "At school, my dad misses a big lacrosse game, so the next day, I get a new computer or God knows what else. They don't have a clue about anything about me." Jay stopped digging and looked at him. "You're the only one who knows who I am." Jay lowered his head, and Don thought he heard him sniffle. "There are times—" Jay began and then cut himself off. "I'd be willing to bet you my new car that if you were to call my dad and ask him where I was, he wouldn't even know, but he'd be arms-deep in some fucking woman's new tits."

The image struck him funny and Don began to laugh, and Jay looked at him for a second like he had two heads. Then he started laughing too. "I'm sorry. I know it's not funny," Don said trying to keep his adolescent sense of humor under control.

"There are lots of times I wish I were you," Jay told him, almost like he was confessing a secret. "You have your mom, and I know you don't have much money." Jay turned to him, looking earnest. "But what you have is so much more important." Jay turned away, and they fell silent.

"You know," Don said eventually, "I was wondering if you'd like to take a walk up to the lighthouse." Jay shrugged an answer. "It's either that, or you'll dig your way to China." Jay's hole had gotten big and the sides were beginning to collapse as it filled with water.

"Okay," Jay agreed, and they packed up their stuff, throwing what they didn't need right away in the car before heading down the beach. They each carried their towels around their necks as they walked. "Sorry for being such a downer," Jay told him.

"Not a biggie. We're all allowed," Don said as he watched a sandpiper skitter through the edge of the waves ahead of them.

The crowd along the beach thinned out, and soon they were walking almost alone with no one around, especially after the land made its sweeping curve toward the point where the lighthouse tower loomed over the sandy hills. "I've always loved this spot," Don said as they stood in the shadow of the tower, looking out over the open ocean. "When I was a kid, I used to ask my mom to bring me here. I never told her, but I used to look for my dad. I'd sometimes dream that I'd see his boat coming in. I knew it wasn't going to happen, but I'd still wish for it anyway." As he talked, the only other people around walked back down the beach, and Jay stroked his cheek before kissing him.

"I wish your dad had come back. As useless as mine can be most of the time, I'm still glad I have the old boobmaster." Jay began to laugh, and Don smacked him lightly on the shoulder before returning the kiss.

Voices floating on the wind broke them apart, and soon a small group of tourists walked toward them. Seeing what they'd wanted to see, Don took a few steps back toward where they'd come from, but Jay tugged him in the other direction, and they began walking farther, up the other side of the island. The inland side was wooded, and Jay led him into the trees just off the beach and kissed him hard. Then Jay tugged the towel from around his neck, setting both their towels on the ground before pulling Don to him until their chests pressed together, and Don could feel Jay's dick against his hip.

Jay tasted a bit like their lunch and sweet like the soda, but mostly he tasted like Jay. As Don opened his mouth, Jay's tongue traced the edge of his lips before darting inside, tasting him. Don tried to get closer, if that was possible, and he felt Jay's hands smooth down his back before resting on his butt, mashing their hips together. "Jay," Don whimpered softly into the kiss, and he felt his swimsuit slide down his hips, Jay's hands pressing it lower until it crumpled around his ankles.

"You're amazing, Donny," Jay whispered into his ear, and Don felt the fabric of Jay's suit move away, and then they were skin to skin, his cock rubbing against Jay's hip. Don could hardly breathe—it felt so good. His hips began to move, and he felt Jay's doing the same thing. Then Jay pressed him back and Don felt the bark of a tree, rough, but not painful.

"God, Jay," he whispered as Jay's lips slipped away from his and he felt Jay's tongue and lips licking along his neck.

"You taste good, Donny, like sunshine and oranges." Jay licked some more before kissing him again and then he was gone. Don tried to catch his breath as Jay spread a towel in front of him. He dared not hope what that meant, but then Jay knelt on it, and Don felt warm wetness slide down him.

"Jesus, Jay," Don gasped, clasping his hands around the tree to steady himself as Jay slid his lips down his shaft, taking more of him into his mouth. He could barely stand it, and Jay had only just touched him. Don tried not to buck his hips, but he couldn't stop it, and as soon as he moved, everything kicked up a notch. He felt and saw Jay bob his head. Don let go of the tree to hold

Jay's shoulders, and then stroked his skin as Jay took him halfway to heaven. Don's balls were already tingling, and he felt Jay touch them lightly, increasing the sensation. "I can't hold it, Jay," he whispered through clenched teeth before giving up and letting go, falling over the edge and into pleasure that up till now he'd only guessed existed.

Resting his head back against the tree, Don kept his eyes closed as he tried to process what had just happened. Looking down at Jay, he saw his best friend's smile, and in that second, Don knew Jay wasn't just his best friend, but someone he loved very much. When Jay stood, Don tugged them together, kissing Jay hard, trying to communicate what he was feeling through the kiss because words seemed to fail him. "I love you" seemed inadequate and too ordinary to say to someone who completely rocked his world off its foundation, who'd opened him to so many things, and who had showed him just how wonderful things could be. No, mere words didn't work at all.

They kissed for a long time, until Don's mind cleared. Then he desperately wanted Jay—he needed him. Kneeling on the towel, he tugged Jay down, laying him out, looking at his powerful body before kissing a trail along Jay's chest.

He hadn't known quite what to expect, but Jay seemed so much *more* than he had in the past. His skin was richer, the flavor headier as Don swirled a tongue around a pink nipple, moving his hand to feel the coarse hair of Jay's groin before curling around the base of his cock and stroking the way he liked on himself. "Donny, please," Jay begged, and Don licked a trail down his stomach to the tip of Jay's cock before sliding his lips over the thick head.

The flavor Don had tasted on Jay's skin burst onto his tongue, and Don wanted more, needed more. Sucking harder, he took more of Jay into his mouth, trying to be careful. Jay was making these high-pitched little noises that told Don he must be

41

doing something right. Then he did what Jay had done to him, bobbing his head slowly.

"Yes, Donny, yes," Jay muttered, and he felt Jay's hands rest on his head as he continued. After a few minutes, he thought he might be getting the hang of it and became bolder, taking Jay deeper and using his tongue along the bottom of the shaft. That must have been good, because Jay started muttering more urgently. Jay's flavor became more intense as Don continued, and Don relished it and the sounds he was hearing because Don knew Jay was making those noises for him, because of him.

Jay's thrusts became ragged, and Don heard him gasp and murmur something just before he filled Don's mouth. Don swallowed, the salty bitterness of Jay's release bursting on his tongue. Don swallowed again, and Jay collapsed back onto the towel, his cock slipping from Don's lips. Don watched as Jay heaved for breath, taking in his flushed cheeks and the open-mouthed awe he saw in Jay's eyes.

"Have you ever done that before?" Jay asked, and Don shook his head. Jay already knew that answer and Don was about to say so, but he realized that Jay meant it as a compliment.

"Have you?" Don asked, and Jay likewise shook his head before flashing a patented Jason grin and sitting up to kiss him. Don returned the kiss, but slowly self-consciousness set in as he became aware that he was bare-naked in the woods. "We should get back," Don said, and Jay nodded before getting to his feet. They both found their suits, and after pulling them on, Jay tugged him into another kiss.

"I love you, Donny," Jay told him. "You're better than my best friend, you're everything." Leave it to Jay to somehow come up with the right words, because all Don could do was hold Jay and nod over and over.

"I love you too," Don managed to say and continued to hold Jay. Finally, he forced himself to let go, and they picked up their towels, shaking them out before walking back along the beach.

By the time they reached the bathing area, the crowd had begun to thin. They decided to take one last swim before heading back. The cool water felt good on Don's sun-heated skin, but he spent most of the time sitting in the shallows watching Jay as he darted and swam through the water. He had so much energy and looked so happy as he played. After a while, Jay came out of the water, but just long enough to pull Don back in for another splash. Then they both got out and went to change clothes.

After throwing their wet things in a bag in the trunk, they pulled out of the parking lot and rode back to town with the windows down. It wasn't long before they were both singing along with the radio—badly, since neither could carry a tune— but it didn't seem to matter to them. Don hadn't felt so happy in a long time. He realized it wasn't just the sex, but being close to another person and having them share something special with him. He'd realized he wasn't the only gay kid in the world, but to have found someone he wanted to spend as much time with as possible and to know that Jay felt the same way about him made Don's heart sing, and he felt like there was nothing that could ruin this day for him. "What do you want to do next?" Jay asked him, and Don smiled and shook his head, the wind whipping through his hair.

"No idea," Don said, not really caring what they did as long as they did it together.

"Let's go play that video game of yours after we get some food," Jay said with a huge grin before turning off the main road. That was another thing they had in common—Jay always seemed to know when Don was hungry, even if he wasn't hungry himself. There was no fast food on the island, so Jay pulled into Mr. Whippy, and they ordered the best hamburgers on the island, with fries, finishing it off with ice cream that they made Don scoop himself, but he didn't mind. He was having a good time.

Once they'd finished, Jay drove them back to the house, where they hung up their wet things on the line before going inside and sitting in Don's small bedroom in front of his computer. Don started the game and then got up so Jay could play. "Where did you get the idea for these crabs?" Jay asked once he had his bait and was dangling it into the water. "I love them. They move perfectly and the colors are so fun." Jay continued playing, swearing occasionally as the crabs got smarter and began stealing the bait and getting out of the trap.

"You have to think like you were really crabbing. Remember how I checked the cage twice, just to be sure? That's what you have to do so the crafty crabs won't get it open," Don explained as Jay groaned, another crab getting away with the goods.

"How does it end?" Jay asked as he continued playing until he'd run out of bait. "Is there an end?"

Don grinned. "There's an end. If you catch all the crabs, and there is a finite number of them, then you definitely win, or if you let the crabs get too smart, then you become the bait." Don smiled as Jay proceeded to test the losing option, and he groaned as the crabs bounded out of the water, latched onto him, and started pinching, making the character roll and squeal, before carrying him back into the water, where he disappeared. At that point the game ended, and Jay whooped and laughed.

"It's amazing, Donny. The technology you used is really cool, but the graphics and the artistry are really great too. I love the way you made the crabs cartoony, but not too cartoony. They actually look sort of menacing." Jay sat back and looked at the screen. "I can't believe you did this all by yourself."

Don shrugged and sat on the edge of the bed. "I just used my imagination. When I was little, I used to think the crabs would get me. I found out quickly that they wouldn't, but I built that into the game for fun." Don watched as Jay turned in the chair.

"What made you think of this?" he asked.

"You did," Don answered. "Once you left last summer, I thought I'd lost my only friend. I was feeling really alone, and my mother told me to do something with the computer. I found the graphics program, and I figured I'd make some sort of picture with the crabs, and it sort of grew from there. I spent a lot of the winter working on it. The hardest part was figuring out how to make the crabs actually get smarter without just making them faster."

"I was wondering about that," Jay said, looking back at the screen.

"What I did was make them more sensitive, so that later in the game you have to get just the right bait in just the right place. They also move a little faster, and they're more aggressive as the game continues. I just had to work out how they all come together, and I figured out the formula just this morning. I can still tweak it, but I really like the way it's working. You can have fun with it when you first pick it up, and as you get further into it, the game becomes more and more challenging." Don was pretty proud of it, and he was even happier that Jay liked it.

"I should head home. My mom is supposed to come back sometime this evening." Jay rolled his eyes as he walked toward the bedroom door before turning around. He walked back and kissed Don hard. "I don't want to go, but Mom will be a pain if I'm not home to spend some 'quality time' with her." Jay's lips devoured him in a kiss that had Don's head swimming. "I'll stop by Mr. Whippy for lunch tomorrow." Jay kissed him once again, and Don wanted to grab Jay, maneuver him onto the bed, and have his way with him, but instead he let him go, very reluctantly. Don watched Jay leave and then heard the door close before going back to work at the computer.

Don tried to do a little work to tune up his game. He had some additional ideas he wanted to try, but his mind wouldn't settle on anything but Jay, what they'd done together, and how he felt. He almost felt as though he were floating on air. He'd wanted to ask Jay about spending the night, but that hadn't worked out. They had the entire summer to spend together, though. In his adolescent mind, he knew that Jay would eventually have to leave, but that was months from now. Opening his e-mail program, he waited for the telephone line to connect and then checked to see if there were any new e-mails. Sure enough, there was one from Jay telling him that his mother was there. Don could almost see Jay rolling his eyes when he mentioned his mother. "I already miss you, D."

Don answered the e-mail, telling Jay that he missed him too. He wanted to say more, but he heard a car pull up outside the house, so he sent his message and then deleted the one from Jay before closing the program. After making sure everything was saved, he walked to the back door and was surprised to see his mother climbing the steps. "Aren't you working?"

She lifted her gaze to him, and Don nearly gasped out loud. She looked tired and drawn, like she'd had a shock. Opening the door, Don hurried down the stairs and helped her up and into the house. "Are you sick?" He was already thinking about what he'd need to do to take care of her.

"Mr. Rodriguez at the store sent me home because he was worried about me," she said as Don helped her into a chair. "After I finished at the restaurant, I had an appointment, and I was supposed to work at the store, but…." She seemed to be babbling a little, and Don's worry ramped up. His mother never missed work and she never got sick—other than the cough she'd had for a while.

"Do you need something to eat?" Don asked, already walking toward the kitchen. He got out a pan and began making scrambled eggs and toast. He put together the plate and brought it to her. Don watched as she sat quietly, picking at the food before setting it aside. "You need to eat, Mom," Don coaxed, and she picked up the plate indulgently and ate a few more bites before setting it aside once again. He knew something was wrong, and he settled in one of the chairs, hoping his mother would tell him. He watched his mother's eyes and saw what almost appeared to be a war going on behind them. Finally, she sighed softly and settled back in the chair.

"You know I've had this cough for a while, and I knew it was nothing, but you kept hounding me to see a doctor. So I did, last week."

Don stared at her, anger welling inside him. "Why didn't you tell me? What did he say?" Don scooted forward in the faded green chair. "Is there something wrong?" The questions would have kept coming, but she patted his hand to quiet him.

"They didn't tell me anything, but they ran some tests and things, and they asked me to come back today." His mother began coughing, and Don got her a glass of water. She drank and settled once again.

"What did they say?" Don could feel himself tensing up when his mother didn't answer right away. "I need to know, Mom."

She shook her head, and then Don saw her do something he'd only ever seen once before—at his father's funeral. She put her hands over her face and began to cry silently. Don saw her shoulders heave up and down as she tried to get herself under control. Don was out of his seat in a flash, his arms around her

47

before he had a chance to think. "It'll be all right, Mom," he said, because he didn't know what else to say as he fought his own tears.

He held her for a while until she began to speak again. "They found a tumor in one of my lungs. They think it's cancer," she told him, and it felt to Don like the entire world stopped spinning. What had been vivid colors all day because of Jay had suddenly turned to shades of black and white. He saw his mother wipe her face, and Don stepped back from her but continued holding her hand. He told himself it was because she needed it, but really, he wanted to grasp onto her and never let her go. "I have an appointment with another doctor next week. The doctor I saw today said that the tumor appears to be one they can operate on and remove, but he wants the opinion of a specialist." Don heard his mother's voice falter once again. "I have no idea how we're going to pay for any of this."

"God, Mom," was all that came out of Don's mouth, and then he was hugging her again. He felt her hand on his head, softly stroking his hair.

"It'll be okay, somehow it'll be okay," she told him, but Don didn't believe it. "No matter what, I'll always be there for you somehow." Don squeezed his eyes shut, but the tears came anyway. He tried to hold them back, but he couldn't stop them. "We're going to be fine, Donny." She patted him on the shoulder a few times. "I know this is a shock, but we've been through worse, and we'll get through this." Don moved away and stood up. "Go on to bed now, honey. You have to get up for work in the morning."

Don nodded absently and walked toward his bedroom, closing the door. He knew he wasn't going to be able to sleep, and he ended up at the computer. There was another message from Jay, and he opened it, but the words seemed to float on the page. Not knowing who else to reach out to, Don typed a single sentence, four words, and pressed send. There was no response.

Don kept looking at the screen, but he didn't get an answer. He wanted to think that Jay had turned off his computer, but Jay's message had come in just a few minutes before Don had sent his. Feeling a bit alone, Don turned off the computer and stared out the window. After looking at nothing for a while, he saw headlight beams sweep across the yard and then go out. He heard an engine shut off and then footsteps on the stairs. Walking quietly through the house, knowing his mother was in her room, Don opened the back door and stepped outside.

He was immediately engulfed in a hug that could only come from Jay. "I got your message and hurried over here," Jay whispered, still holding him tight.

He heard a window slide open, and Jay released him, allowing Don to step back. "Donny, is that you?"

"Yes. I'm with Jay," he answered, hearing the window close again as the old air-conditioner fan started up with its usual wheezing sound.

"Come on," Jay said, and Don followed him down the steps and out behind the old shed, where they sat on the warm ground, and Jay once again pulled him close in the darkness. "What happened?" Jay whispered.

Don told Jay what little he knew in a soft voice so no one could overhear. "She has to go to a different doctor next week." He didn't know that much, but what he did scared the hell out of him. "What if she dies, Jay? What if they can't get it and she dies?" Don felt the tears come again as he thought of a life without her. She had always been there for him, just like the mothers in the bedtime stories she used to read to him when he was little. The thought of her not being there made him wish the earth would open and swallow him up.

"I wish I could tell you it's going to be okay, but I don't know, either," Jay said softly, and Don clung to him, needing someone. The person he'd usually take his troubles to was going through something worse than he was. Resting his head on Jay's shoulder, he quietly began to cry as fear took hold of him.

"I'm sorry I'm being such a wuss," Don murmured against Jay's shoulder, but the response he got was to be held tighter.

"There's nothing wussy about being sad or afraid to lose the people who love you," Jay told him as he stroked along Don's back. "You're allowed to be scared, but you have to be strong for your mother." Don knew Jay was right, and he lifted his head. In the darkness, he could just make out Jay's face. "Your mother is going to need you to be there for her the way she's always been there for you." Don nodded slowly, and Jay ran his hand along his cheek.

"I know, but how?" He really didn't expect Jay to have the answers. Don was already trying to think of possible ways to make money. He knew, if nothing else, that his mother was going to be off work for a while. They could barely make ends meet with her working two jobs and him working as well. They both knew they had to put money aside, because the winter months were really lean. His mom being sick was going to mean a very long winter.

"All you can do is help her any way you can. Your mom will probably have surgery and then treatments to make sure all the cancer is gone. Those can be the hardest part, depending on what they think they'll need to do," Jay told him, and Don slowly nodded, his head facing down onto his lap. "I love ya, Don, and I'll help too, if I can."

Don didn't know what Jay could do, but the simple offer of help made him feel better. He didn't really expect any, but the support meant the world. "I love you too," Don said, taking a deep breath. He had to be the man of the house now in more ways than just in name. Up to now, he'd helped his mother, but she did most of the work and still took care of him. Now he had to take care of her. "Thanks, Jay."

"For what?" he asked.

"Being there," Don said. "When I sent the note and you didn't answer, I thought…. And then you'd rushed over." Don felt his emotions bubbling to the surface again.

"It's okay," Jay whispered again and then leaned closer, and Don felt Jay kiss him. Earlier in the day their kisses had been deep, exploring and tasting, but this kiss was so soft and tender that Don nearly started crying again, and once it ended, Don blinked a few times but failed to keep the tears at bay. Jay stood up and took his hand, pulling Don to his feet. "I need to get home or my mother will pitch a fit. She's suddenly acting all motherly and weird, but I'll see you tomorrow, I promise." Jay kissed him in the darkness once again before walking to his car. When he opened the door, Don saw him wave, and then he climbed in. Don waited as the engine started, and then the headlights swept the yard again. Don waited until the sound of the car faded into the distance before going in the house.

He walked quietly through the dark house. He hoped his mother was asleep as he closed the door to his bedroom and got ready for bed before climbing between the sheets. He tried to sleep but ended up staring at his ceiling, worrying until he finally fell asleep.

DAY 3

LATER THAT SUMMER
CHINCOTEAGUE ISLAND, VA

DON'S alarm sounded, but he was already awake, and he silenced it and got out of bed. Not making a sound, he cleaned up and dressed before going into the kitchen. He made a light breakfast for himself and then fixed a small plate. Walking down the hall, he carried the plate and a small glass of juice to his mother's room. Carefully opening the door, he saw his mother curled under the blankets, but knew she was awake. "I have something for you to eat," he said softly, and she began to sit up. It took a minute, which Don knew was because sudden movements messed with her balance. Once she was up, he set the plate in front of his mother, and she slowly began to eat.

"Tastes good today," she said softly, and Don breathed a sigh of relief.

"How's your breathing?" Don asked, and his mother inhaled and exhaled without coughing before actually smiling at him.

"It's a lot better," she answered. "They said I'd feel better once the tumor was gone, and I finally do." Don turned on a small light and noticed that she looked better. For the first time in almost two months, he let himself breathe a small sigh of relief.

Once the cancer diagnosis had been confirmed, everything had moved very fast. Surgery had been scheduled, and his mother had been admitted to the hospital right away. They said the actual tumor wasn't as large as they'd feared, so that was good. At first they were afraid they would need to take a large part of one of her lungs, but the smaller tumor had been a blessing, and they were able to save much of his mother's right lung. They also felt that the cancer had remained localized and that they'd gotten it all. Because of its location, the doctor didn't feel that chemotherapy would be beneficial, but he did prescribe a course of radiation treatments. So each week they traveled to the hospital for her treatment. For two days afterward, she'd be confined to bed, sleeping. All food made her nauseous and light bothered her. Then she'd start to feel better. By the end of the week, she'd start to feel good, and then it was time for another treatment. She'd been enduring these treatments for four weeks, and she had eight more to go. His mother finished eating and then slowly pushed back the covers and got out of bed.

"Should you be up?" Don asked, wanting her to go back to bed and rest.

"I need to get some things done so I can go to work tomorrow. Besides, I'm feeling pretty good." She flashed Don a look that said not to argue, so instead, he took the dishes and left the room. In the kitchen, he washed and dried the dishes, making sure everything was cleaned up. "Are you working today?"

"No. I was going to stay here and help you," Don answered, but his mother shook her head.

"Go have some fun and get out of this house," she told him, and Don didn't wait to ask if she was sure. Instead, he picked up the phone, dialed Jay's number, and waited for him to answer.

"How's your mom?" Jay asked as soon as he realized who was calling.

"She seems to be doing better. Mom ate pretty well and doesn't seem to be so tired. Since I have the day off, she told me to get out of the house, so I was wondering if you'd like to do something." They'd spent a lot of time together. Mostly watching movies and stuff at his house, because there had been a lot of times when he didn't feel he could leave his mom alone. Jay had been great through it all. When his mom had been in surgery, Jay had sat with him the entire time.

"You could come over here," Jay offered. "My mom's gone for the day, and we can play video games. I also got some crabbing stuff, and I asked Mom to pick up chicken necks at the store." Jay began to laugh. "You should have seen the look on her face."

"Great, I'll see you in a while," Don agreed before hanging up.

"Now that's something I haven't seen in a long time," his mother commented as he walked toward his bedroom. "It's been a long time since you've smiled like that." She continued looking at him and seemed about to say something, but turned away instead. "You two have fun, and I'll see you for dinner."

Don gave her a gentle hug before hurrying out the back door. He got his bike out of the shed, locked the doors again and took off toward Jay's as fast as his legs could pump the pedals. As he passed Mr. Winters's place, he slowed and waved to Mr. Winters before continuing on.

Jay was obviously looking for him because he was already hurrying down the stairs as Don pulled up. After coasting to a stop, he leaned his bike against one of the pilings and followed Jay back up the stairs into the house. Jay closed the door, and then Don found himself pressed back against it, Jay kissing him hard. "I missed you so bad," Jay said before kissing him again. Don forgot all about going crabbing, or anything else, for that matter, as Jay pulled his shirt up, breaking the kiss only long enough to get their shirts off.

"I missed you too," Don said, and Jay's eyes met his. He'd felt guilty for weeks because he hadn't had much time to spend alone with Jay, but the look in Jay's eyes told him he had nothing to feel guilty about. Jay understood. "It's been so long," Don murmured as he threw his arms around Jay's neck, pulling him in for another kiss.

"Come on," Jay said, breaking away and scooping their shirts off the floor before taking him by the hand and leading him through the house to his bedroom. Don laughed as Jay tackled him in a hug that ended with both of them bouncing on the bed. "I'm glad your mom is doing better," Jay began, and Don groaned.

"Let's not talk about my mother while you're trying to get at my stuff. It sort of kills the mood," Don said with a chuckle that turned into a full-on laugh as Jay tickled along his ribs. Don forgot about everything except Jay's hands on his skin, and once the tickling ended, the kissing and touching began in earnest. Don gazed up into Jay's eyes and watched them go from playful to serious and languid within the pace of a few seconds. He really didn't have the words to describe it himself, but in his mind, he always referred to this look on Jay's face as his sexy expression because it was the one Jay got whenever they were together like this. That look never failed to make Don tingle. He loved it when Jay looked at him that way because he knew in his heart that Jay never looked at anyone else like that. He'd seen Jay with many people in many situations, and that expression was only for him.

"Does this kill the mood?" Jay teased as he tugged off Don's jeans, dropping them on the floor. Don shook his head and squirmed as Jay continued gazing at him. He always thought he looked skinny, especially compared to Jay. Whenever he undressed with Jay, Don always wanted to hide under the covers, not because of anything Jay had ever said or done, but because he always thought his body paled in comparison to Jay's. "What's wrong?" Jay asked, pulling him out of his woolgathering.

"Nothing," Don answered. "I was just thinking about the look you were giving me."

"You mean the 'Don is so sexy I want to watch him forever' look? Because I do. I know you see yourself as skinny, or whatever you told me once, but I see you as you. You are who you are, and that's pretty amazing to me." Jay leaned down, licking across his belly in one long, hot swipe of his tongue. "You taste like the sunshine and the ocean, and… you. Best flavor there is." Jay licked circles around one of his nipples, and Don squirmed at the zing of pleasure. "Never let anyone make you feel less than you are, because they're just full of it. You're pretty amazing, Donald Pottier, and I should know, because I could never love anyone who wasn't totally amazingly wonderful." Jay grinned at him before crashing their mouths together in a kiss that Don was sure was designed to keep him from arguing, and damn if it didn't succeed.

Don squirmed under the onslaught of Jay's kiss—there was so much energy and need in it that Don's brain began to short-circuit a little in the most amazing way. He held Jay and let him take control. Jay was strong, and Don trusted him completely; that feeling added to his own passion. Jay always took care of him, and Don let him do that once again. Jay tugged away his shorts, and soon Jay was naked as well, their hot bodies coming together in a blaze of passion. "I need you, Jay," Don muttered, and in return he got a kiss that threatened to stand his unruly hair on end.

"I know," Jay responded, his mouth just above Don's, so close Don could feel his breath on his lips. "I need you too." Jay hugged him tight, pressing him between the mattress and his body, their dicks throbbing and sliding past each other.

"I'm sorry I haven't... I'm sorry," Don muttered.

Jay didn't say anything for a long time, and Don began to squirm. "You have nothing to be sorry for. I wish more than anything I had a family like yours. You really care about one another and would do anything for each other." Jay began to shake, and Don quickly realized that Jay wasn't being sexy anymore. "I hate them," Jay said as he rolled onto the mattress. "I just hate them." Jay lay on the bed, his hands over his face. "They want to run my life but not have anything to do with me," Jay screamed into the room, and Don watched as Jay continued shaking. "My dad has decided what college he wants me to go to, and he's even picked my career for me. The man doesn't even know me, Donny, and he wants to run my life."

Don didn't know quite how to respond at first, and he stared at Jay for a few moments. "My mom is fighting cancer, and you're angry because your dad wants to choose your college? Fine, Jay, your dad can choose my college for me if he wants. I'll even let him choose my career if it means I can have one." Don sat up before staring Jay in the face. "Knock it off and quit whining, Jay. That's probably his way of showing he cares. Did you ever make an effort to get to know him? You told me once that I needed to step up and help my mom. Well, maybe you need to do the same with your dad. Get to know him. Maybe you'll find out he's as big a dick as you think he is, but maybe you'll find out he's a great guy who hasn't known what to do all these years." Don slid off the bed and began pulling on his clothes.

"Where are you going?" Jay asked, leaping off the mattress and hugging him tight.

Don shrugged. "I don't know. You have so many advantages, and instead of using them, you just get angry." Don turned to face him. "I love you, Jay, but I'm so jealous of you I could scream. You get to go to college, you get to have a life in the world, you'll get the chance to make all your dreams come true and have more opportunities than I could ever dream of. Be grateful for what you have, because it could be gone." Don dropped the clothes he was carrying, and Jay pulled him toward the bed. He felt a bit foolish standing naked in Jay's bedroom crying like a baby, but that was what he was doing.

"I should be grateful for what I have," Jay said softly, and then Don felt himself being tugged onto the bed and into Jay's arms. "I have you."

"Isn't that a little corny?" Don asked.

"Only if it's not true," Jay told him, and then Don was prone on the bed with Jay covering him and kissing him, but this time it was different. Some of the raw energy was gone, replaced with caresses that were deeper and less hurried. "I want you, Donny," Jay said, his voice deepening, and at first Don wasn't sure what Jay meant. Then his eyes widened, and he realized what Jay was asking. "I want to be with you."

"I want that too," Don answered. "But I don't know what to do." He felt like such a baby. He loved Jay so much. "Will it hurt?"

Jay's eyes locked on his, and Don realized Jay didn't know the answer. "I'd never hurt you."

Don wished that were true. He knew that in a few weeks Jay was going to leave, and that was going to hurt. It wasn't Jay's fault, but that didn't matter, because Don was going to feel pain when Jay left. He knew there was no way around it, but he also knew he wanted to give Jay everything he could and have as many memories as possible. Lifting his legs, Don wrapped them around Jay's waist, opening himself, and he heard Jay groan softly.

Warm, loving hands caressed down his thighs, fingers ghosting over his opening, a place that only he had ever touched. Jay's fingers felt so good. Don tried to keep his eyes open, locking them on Jay's, but he wasn't able to as Jay teased his tender, sensitive flesh. "I need something," Jay said, and Don stilled, wondering what they needed. He felt Jay shift, reaching next to the bed, and after opening and closing a drawer, he returned with what looked like a small bottle. "It's unscented massage oil."

Don waited as he watched Jay open the bottle and squeezed a little on his fingers. When Jay's hands returned to his skin, they felt warmer and softer, and the feel of Jay's fingers on his opening had him vibrating with excitement. He'd wondered a few times what this would feel like, and he'd hoped that someday he and Jay might share this. "It's good."

Jay swirled a finger around his opening, and then Don held his breath, holding back a tiny gasp as the tip of Jay's finger slipped inside him. He'd thought it might hurt, but it felt really good, and slowly, Jay sank deeper into him. He felt Jay's finger moving, and then Jay touched a spot inside him, and small lights flashed behind Don's eyes.

"Jay!" he cried, not quite sure what was happening to him. "Do that again." His skin seemed more sensitive and Jay's touch more alive. He wasn't sure what had happened, but he liked it. Hell, he loved it. Jay touched that place again, rubbing in little circles, and Don could barely breathe. His dick throbbed and jumped between their bodies, and he knew he was saying all kinds of stuff, but his mouth seemed to have developed a mind of its own.

Jay withdrew his finger and added another, stretching him. He felt a slight burning sensation at first, but that quickly passed and he felt really full. When Jay added another finger, he gasped and held still, not sure he could take it, but the initial pain melted away. "I can't wait any longer, Donny," Jay told him, and Don nodded. He felt the fingers slip out of him, and Jay opened the oil again.

Don was definitely nervous, and when he felt Jay press against him, every muscle in his body clenched. "It's okay," Jay crooned to him, "I'll never hurt you. Relax and remember how my fingers felt."

Don made his muscles relax, and Jay slipped inside him. At first, Don wasn't too sure if he liked it, but the pain and funny stretching feeling passed, and he realized that Jay, his Jay, was inside him. Don breathed slowly and deeply as he felt Jay press deeper inside him. "Please stop," he cried, and Jay stilled completely.

"What's wrong?"

Before Don could answer, he felt Jay beginning to pull out. "Stop, Jay. I just want to feel you for a second." Don needed a minute to get used to the myriad of new and different feelings that were happening inside him. "Move slowly," Don told Jay, and Jay got this funny look on his face. "What?"

"You're pushy in bed," Jay said with a smile that slipped away as he pressed deeper into him. "God, you can be as pushy as you want." Jay sounded breathless, and Don could feel his cock jumping inside him. Then he felt Jay's hips against his butt, and they both stilled as Don tried to catch his breath. Jay's head lolled back. "You feel incredible around me. It's hard to describe." Jay withdrew slowly, and Don's eyes bugged. "Okay?"

"Hell, yes," Don moaned, and Jay continued moving. He knew this was probably a bit of a comedy of errors, but every time Jay moved, it felt so dang good, and he just wanted to savor it. "This is our first time," he told Jay with a smile.

"I'm glad it's with you," Jay said as he began to move again. This time Don knew what to expect, and Jay began moving faster. He could feel their bodies and instinct taking over. Everything around him faded as Don concentrated on every move Jay made and everything he made him feel. For a while, Don felt as though this was too good to be true and Jay had to be making love to someone else, but he wasn't. Jay was here with him, loving him.

Don tugged Jay down into a kiss, sloppy and ragged, but Don didn't care as Jay's tongue filled his mouth the way his cock filled his ass. He wanted to taste and feel Jay in every way possible. Something deep inside him said to make the most of the time they had because Jay was going to leave soon. And next summer they wouldn't be kids anymore, but men, and Don knew that would change things forever. They couldn't stop it if they tried.

"What's wrong?" Jay asked him. "You're thinking too much." Don pulled him into another kiss as their passion ramped up, driving all wayward thoughts from Don's mind.

He stroked himself as Jay drove into him, Don's body begging for a release that Jay wasn't ready to give him. Just when he thought he'd reached the peak, Jay would drive it higher. Don gasped and cried out when Jay moved Don's hand away and stroked his length, hard and fast, moving his hand in time to the cock buried deep inside him. "Can't hold it, Jay!"

"Don't," Jay commanded, and Don fell over the edge, coming in a blinding flash as he screamed his release. He felt like he didn't have control of his own body and just rode the waves of pleasure that Jay had built for him. Don came back to himself just in time to watch as Jay came undone before his eyes, his mouth open, his head thrown back. Jay snapped his hips forward, every muscle in his body as taut as a bowstring, and then Don felt Jay's release overtake him. He felt every pulse Jay made deep inside him, the jumps of his cock, the throbbing and pumping as Jay flooded him with heat. He watched as Jay gasped for breath and then collapsed on top of him, and Don soothed and caressed his lover's damp skin.

"I missed you, Jay," Don said softly, and he felt Jay nod a little.

"I missed spending more time with you too," Jay told him. "But I understand."

"With my mom feeling better, we can spend most of the next couple weeks together," Don whispered, and Jay lifted his head and smiled.

"I'd like that," Jay answered before burying his face in Don's shoulder. He could feel Jay kissing his skin as their bodies disconnected with a ping of hypersensation that sent a shudder through Don's body. "To celebrate that, how about we clean up and then go crabbing like we used to." Jay lifted Don's face, brushing the errant hairs away from his forehead to look into his eyes.

"Yes, let's do that, and if we catch enough, I bet we can get my mom to help us make crab cakes," Don said, and he saw Jay's eyes glaze over and heard his stomach rumble, followed by Jay's infectious laugh.

"Let's clean up, and then we can eat before we waste away to nothing," Jay quipped, climbing gingerly off the bed. Don followed him into the bathroom, and Jay started the shower.

Don's body still tingled as he stepped under the spray with Jay behind him. As the water ran down his chest and stomach, Jay wrapped his arms around his chest, his body pressing to Don's back, head resting on his shoulder. "What are we going to do, Donny?" Jay asked, his voice barely loud enough to carry over the sound of the water. "I have to leave in a few weeks. I expect to be back next summer, but I don't want to wait that long to see you." Jay made small circles with his hands on Don's skin, and Don leaned back into the touch, remaining quiet because he didn't have any answers. "I thought that maybe I could ask if I could come back during spring break."

Don turned in Jay's arms, feeling like his heart was already breaking even though Jay was still here. "I don't know. I'd love if you could come back to visit, but you'll have school and your friends." Don smoothed the hair away from Jay's forehead. "We graduate from high school next year, and our lives are going to take us away from each other. You know that." There was no way he could go to college or leave the island, or his mother, for that matter. He was tied here, caged here like one of the crabs they caught.

Jay scowled at him. "Is that what you want?" Jay asked accusingly, stepping away.

"No, it's not what I want, but it's what will happen." Don tried to keep his sadness out of his voice and was grateful that the shower covered most of it. "You'll graduate and go on to college, and I'll graduate and stay here. Maybe I can come to Chicago to be near you, but what will I do? Work at McDonald's or as a waiter in a restaurant? I have no future, and you have the entire world in front of you. You can do anything and be anything you want. And I want that for you, I want you to take on the world and make it a better place."

Jay was shaking his head. "That's what I want for *you*. You're the one who's going to take on the world. I have a father with money, but you have an amazing talent, and soon someone besides me is going to recognize it." Jay reached for the soap, and Don felt Jay's hands soap his skin. "I don't want you to give up hope or stop making your games and anything else you want to do. You have to promise me."

Don had no idea why this was so important to Jay. "I promise," he said, not thinking any more about it as he turned around and let Jay wash his back.

"And I promise that somehow I'll come back to see you. I'm not sure how I'll do it, but I will." Jay turned him again, the water washing away the soap, and Jay squirted a dollop of shampoo into his hand.

"Jay, don't make promises you may not be able to keep," Don said as Jay began washing his hair. "I know you love me, and I know you'll try to come back to see me. That's enough." It had to be. Don couldn't allow himself to hope too much because he knew it would only lead to heartache and broken dreams. He closed his eyes, relishing the feel of Jay's hands in his hair, the warm water rinsing away the lather. Reaching out, he ran his hands over Jay's skin. Even with his eyes closed, he could almost see Jay as he touched him. Don let his hands roam over Jay's chest, the muscles playing under the skin, rippling and moving beneath his touch, down to his stomach, which fluttered slightly. Then Don lightly stoked Jay's cock, perfect and smooth. He felt it awaken under his touch, hardening in his hand. Without thinking, Don sank to his knees, the water sluicing over him. Not even opening his eyes, Don took Jay into his mouth, experiencing his lover with touch and taste.

"God, Donny," Jay murmured as Don sucked him deeper, Jay's rich muskiness bursting onto his tongue. Don had become quite good at this, as evidenced by the whimpers coming from above him. He felt Jay lean back and knew his lover was against the tile, hands splayed. He'd seen him that way enough to know exactly how Jay loved this and exactly what to do to drive him wild. Pulling his head back, Don tightened his lips around the base of Jay's cockhead and held them there. He could feel Jay trying to move and knew he desperately wanted more. Jay's cock jumped and throbbed between his lips, and still he didn't move. "Donny, please," Jay begged, and he slowly sucked Jay back into his mouth. Don loved the feel of Jay's cock sliding along his tongue and the way it fit just right in the back of his throat when he took it all. Bobbing his head, Don did everything he knew Jay liked, running his tongue along the ridge, taking him deep, and Jay's favorite, filling his mouth with warm water and swishing it around Jay's dick. He almost always came unglued when Don did that, and this time was no exception. "Can't wait," Jay warned, and Don sucked as hard as he could. Jay started to come, and Don swallowed hard as a bang echoed outside the house.

Jay stilled, and Don swallowed the last of his release. Turning off the water, they continued listening for a second, and then Jay stepped out of the shower and grabbed a towel, hurrying out of the bathroom. Don followed and saw him peering out his bedroom window, and then Jay started drying himself off fast. "My mom's here," he whispered, and Don reached for a towel, drying himself as well. "She's talking to the neighbor."

Don nodded and finished drying himself before starting to pull on his clothes. Don got his underwear and pants on by the time he heard the front door close and Jay's mother call up the stairs. Jay was nearly dressed as he hurried to the door. "We're up here, Mom. Don and I are working on the computer," Jay called, and Don looked at the computer, which was sitting on the desk, the screen black. Don finished pulling on his shirt before pushing the on button on the computer. Then he hurried to get his shoes and socks on. Don heard her footsteps on the stairs as he finished dressing, and Jay sat in his desk chair as the computer booted up. He'd just opened a program and had begun typing as the door opened. "Hey, Mom, did you have a good time at the spa?"

Don turned around and saw their towels resting on the floor at the end of the bed. "The usual," she answered, and Don could feel her taking in the room and them. "I brought some things for lunch, so come downstairs in a few minutes to eat."

"Okay, Mom," Jay said, closing the file and standing up. "We'll be right down."

She didn't leave right away, and Don's heart began to pound. Don felt a bit like a deer in headlights. "Be sure to hang up those towels," she said. "I don't want to find them days from now the way I usually do."

"We will, Mom," Jay told her, and Don picked up the towels and walked past her toward the bathroom. "You're such a nice young man," she said as Don passed, and he continued into the bathroom, where he hung up the towels. He also cleaned up a bit before closing the door and returning to Jay's bedroom. His heart still pounded, and Jay looked a bit wide-eyed, as well, but didn't say anything. Don was hoping for some cue from Jay. "Let's go downstairs."

Don followed Jay, and they descended to the main level. Mrs. Greene had set a bunch of containers on the counter, and Jay grabbed a plate and began filling it. Don followed along behind, noticing Mrs. Greene watching him. "What do you two have planned for this afternoon?" she asked before reaching for her purse and pulling out a pack of cigarettes and a lighter. Without waiting for an answer, she opened the large sliding glass doors and stepped onto the deck, closing the door behind her. Jay scowled as she stood outside smoking her cigarette. "She smokes all the time, and your mom is the one who gets lung cancer," Jay said as he opened the refrigerator and brought out two cans of Coke. "It's probably from working in that smoky restaurant all day," he added. Don had long thought that working in that smoky place wasn't good for her, but it was her job, and they needed to eat.

"This is Virginia, tobacco country," Don said off the cuff, because that was the reason he had always been given by his mother whenever he'd asked about it. Jay agreed with a nod before carrying his plate to the table, watching his mother.

They didn't talk much while they ate, but Don kept looking at Jay, feeling a bit uncomfortable. He was getting the feeling that Jay's mother suspected something. She kept looking at him through the glass, and it looked like she didn't want Don to know she was doing it. He'd met Mrs. Greene many times, and she'd always been nice, if a little preoccupied and distant, but this sort of behavior was different. Jay didn't seem to notice anything and continued eating, paying little attention to his mother except to scowl at her as she lit yet another cigarette. "I'm about done," Jay announced, and Don ate the last bite from his own plate. They carried their dishes to the sink. Jay grabbed two more sodas from the refrigerator before opening the glass doors. "We're going crabbing for a while."

Jay closed the glass door, and Don saw the two of them talking, but he couldn't hear what they were saying. Then Jay opened the door again, smiling as he closed it behind him.

"Is something wrong?" Don asked.

Jay laughed. "Nope, she's just being her usual self. Let's go." Jay opened the refrigerator and grabbed a package in white butcher paper before hurrying toward the door. They descended the stairs in a hurry.

"I found a new place," Don told Jay as they gathered the supplies. "It's a walk, but I don't think anyone else crabs there. I caught a bunch there last week and had to let a bunch go because I'd gotten my limit."

"Cool," Jay said with excitement.

"It's past my house, so I'd like to stop a minute to make sure Mom's okay."

"No problem," Jay told him before handing him the cooler and the net. "Let's get going." Jay popped his trunk, and they loaded the things before taking off. They stopped at Don's home, and Don hurried inside. His mom was resting on the sofa, and he didn't disturb her, but he noticed that the house had been cleaned and vacuumed. Satisfied, he left again and got in Jay's car, giving him directions, and when they arrived, he helped Jay find a dry spot to park.

"The wall's old here, but still solid," he explained as he led Jay around a small pool of water to the old seawall. They found a spot behind the wall that was high and dry and began setting up. Both of them were now experts at preparing the bait, and they soon had the chicken necks in the water and the nets nearby. "One of the things I like is that there's shade. I think that's why the crabs are here like this." Don settled on the ground, with Jay sitting next to him.

"Do you ever wonder what it would be like to live someplace else?" Jay asked, looking out over the water.

"All the time," Don answered with a laugh. "And yet things are good here. I can go crabbing most of the summer, fish, and hunt for oysters." Don checked the lines and scooped out a crab, which he put in the cage before lowering it into the water. "I wish there was more opportunity here, though. It's a great place, with the ocean, bays, and inlets. There isn't the noise and chaos of Ocean City." Don wasn't sure where he was going with this or why he was waxing poetic about a place he'd always wished he could leave. "The people here are pretty great too. They're holding a benefit for Mom next month to raise money to help with her medical bills." Don got quiet, listening to the soft lap of the water against the pilings and the seagulls calling as they flew overhead. "This is home, I guess."

Jay checked the lines and they each netted a crab. "This is a good place," Jay told him as he closed the cage before putting it back in the water. "But if you could go anyplace else, where would it be?"

"I don't know," Don answered. "Maybe Paris. I saw pictures in a book once, and it looked so beautiful, like a fairytale place. But that could have been just the pictures." Don sat back down, knowing it didn't really matter how he answered—he wasn't going to get to go there. "How about you?"

Jay looked at him. "I've been to Paris, and it wasn't just the pictures. I went with my parents a few years ago."

"But if you could go anywhere," Don prompted, wondering where Jay would choose.

"Maybe Tahiti or Hawaii, someplace tropical and warm with ocean breezes like this, and a house built over the water so you could watch the fish through the floor. Although I'd go anywhere with you." Jay laughed, and Don did too. They were alone, and Don looked around before moving closer to Jay. Their lips met in a soft kiss that had Don instantly hard and ready to go. "We need to be careful," Jay reminded him, and Don pulled back, making a show of checking the lines.

"I wish we had a boat. There are great things to see from a boat."

"That's the one thing my dad won't buy. I asked Mom about it, and she said that my dad's afraid of the water. The beach is as close as he'll get." Jay was actually laughing, and Don found that funny as well. "I was thinking we could take one of the boat trips from town when you get your next day off. It would be fun, and while it isn't our own boat, it would still be a blast."

"Okay," Don answered quickly. He knew most of the captains, and he could probably arrange for a special trip if they went during the week instead of on a weekend. Jay checked the lines again and carefully scooped a crab into the net.

"Look at him. He's huge," Jay cried, fishing the big blue crab out of the net and holding it up. "Wish I had a camera." Jay's smile lit his face, and Don wished they had a camera as well just so he could take Jay's picture with the happy look on his face.

"Biggest one I've ever seen," Don commented with a smile. "It reminds me of the mega-crab from the game. But I don't think he's going to fit in the cage," Don said as he lifted it out of the water. He opened the door, and Jay had to turn the crab diagonally, but he got it inside.

As the afternoon wore on, they caught a number of crabs, and they talked about everything that seemed important at the time. "I think we have enough," Don said as he lifted the cage from the water, the crabs crawling over one another inside it.

"I think you're right," Jay agreed, and they began packing up, walking carefully back to the car.

"Hey Potty-a," a familiar voice called, and Don turned to see Harmon standing near where Jay's car was parked. "Looks like you and your boyfriend caught some crabs. Bet you got them from each other."

"Clever, Crap-ke," Jay retorted. "I bet your pea brain really strained to come up with that one." They put their stuff in the trunk, and Don saw Jay walk to where Harmon stood. "You leave him alone, or I'll kick the shit out of you again." Jay puffed himself up, and Don saw Harmon blanch.

"You're a fag!" Harmon called as he stepped back as Jay approached. "I saw you kissing."

"You saw nothing," Jay hissed as he burst into a run. Harmon took off, and Jay chased him for show and then walked back to the car.

"He'll tell everyone," Don said when Jay returned.

"No one will believe him. You know he's always saying crap about people. You bore the brunt of it for a long time. No one will pay attention to whatever he says as long as we ignore it and don't behave any differently," Jay said, but Don saw him turn to look where Harmon had gone, and when he turned around, he looked worried too. Jay had told him plenty of stories about how his dad felt about gay people. "Let's go back to your house and give your mom what we caught," Jay said, and Don knew he was trying to change the subject. They finished loading the car and rode to Don's, where his mother greeted them from the back door.

"Mrs. Pottier, we caught some good ones," Jay called as they climbed the steps.

"You certainly did," Don's mother said as she took the cage inside. Don pulled out the large pot, running water into it before setting it on the stove. His mother put in her spices, and once the water started to boil, she began placing the crabs in the pot.

Things seemed remarkably like they had before his mother's diagnosis. She had some energy again. Once the crabs were steamed, they cracked them open and she began the process of making her famous crab cakes. Don hadn't had them in months, and it felt good to make and eat something so familiar. At dinner, Jay had praised his mother's cooking the way he always did, and Don felt truly happy. His mother seemed more like herself, and he had Jay to laugh and joke with. When they were done eating, he and Jay shooed his mother out of the kitchen to rest, and they did the dishes, a process that included a lot of laughter and a soap-bubble fight.

"Thank you once again for a great meal, Mrs. Pottier," Jay said to Don's mother, and she actually hugged him.

"You're welcome here any time, you know that," his mother said before adding, "Drive safely."

"I will," Jay told her, and Don walked Jay to his car. "I'll see you tomorrow after you get done with work," Jay said, and Don watched as Jay got in the car and drove away. Like he always did, he waited until Jay's car was out of sight before going back in the house.

THE phone rang half an hour later, and Don hurried to get up from his computer to answer it. "Donny," he heard Jay whisper as soon as he answered.

"Yeah, it's me. What's wrong?" All he heard was what sounded like tears.

"We're leaving tomorrow. My dad got here today and—"

Don heard Jay's dad's voice in the background. "You are not to talk to that boy! Now pack your shit or we'll leave it all."

"I gotta go...," Jay said, and then the phone was slammed down, and Don heard nothing more. He stared at the phone for a few minutes and then placed it back in the cradle before beginning to shake. Jay was leaving tomorrow. Hurrying back to his room, he opened the e-mail program and found a message from Jay that had been sent a few minutes earlier.

> Someone called the house about us, and my dad answered the phone. He just got here, and they're making me pack because we're leaving in the morning. I can't call you, but I couldn't leave without telling you that I love you one more time, and this is the only way I can.

The message ended there. Don read the message again and kept checking to see if there was another, but there wasn't. He typed a message to Jay, telling him he loved him too and was about to send it, but he didn't want to get Jay in any more trouble. Barely thinking, he printed both messages on his printer and placed the sheets in the decorated wooden box Jay had sent him when his family went to Jamaica, setting it on his desk. Afterward, he checked again, but nothing else came.

Don thought about trying to go over to Jay's house, but he didn't know what he would do when he got there, and he expected to be turned away by Jay's parents. He didn't know what to do, but he had to try to see Jay one last time before he left, even if he didn't know how to do it. Getting up, he began to prowl the tiny room, willing his brain to come up with some brilliant plan, but of course nothing came. As he continued walking, his grief and despair began to shift to anger. He had to try, damn it; he had to try something.

After leaving his room, Don walked to the door, each step coming faster until he ran down the steps and out to the shed. He unlocked it with fumbling hands, then yanked out his bike and jumped onto it, his legs pounding as he rode. When he got to the end of the street, he turned toward Jay's and pedaled with everything he had. As he approached Mr. Winters's place, he set his bike near one of the trees and walked the rest of the way, staying out of sight. There was a tremendous amount of activity around the house, people packing and carrying things to the car. Don stayed out of sight, but nearly gasped when he saw the yard littered with what appeared to be the remains of Jay's computer. It looked like someone had thrown it against a tree. Jay's dad charged back up the stairs and then returned, this time followed by Jay, who walked slowly, with his head down. His dad never looked at him or said anything. Jay loaded the things in the other car and returned to the house.

Don willed Jay to look up and see him, but Jay wasn't looking anywhere or at anything but his shoes. Don stayed where he was until no one made any trips anymore. Then the door remained closed, and Don's eyes traveled to the window on the second floor that he knew was Jay's. He saw the light come on and the curtains part. Then he saw Jay's head and face looking out for a few seconds before the window cranked open. Through the downstairs windows, Don could see Jay's folks, and they appeared to be yelling at one another.

"Donny, are you out there?" Don thought he heard from Jay's window. Slowly, he made his way forward, but then stopped when he saw the windows on the first floor open and Jay's father look out. Don stayed behind the tree and continued waiting, but then he heard Jay's dad yelling to him to close the window.

Don watched as Jay's window closed and the light in his room went out. The other windows in the house closed as well. He wished he could get a message to Jay, somehow talk to him one more time, but it didn't appear possible. Slowly, he made his way back through the trees and then down the road to his bike. Getting on, he rode back toward home.

As he got close to the house, Don sped up and didn't pull into his drive, but kept going until he found himself turning, heading to town. He continued pounding the pedals, the bike speeding faster than he'd ever gone, his legs aching, but he barely noticed. Don took corners like a madman, riding up the main street until he saw the pirate miniature golf course. Pulling into the drive, he cut off a car, not giving a fuck if he got hit. He had one goal in mind now, and the anger he'd felt earlier had built with every passing second and every heaving downward thrust of his pedals.

The bike had barely come to a stop on the sidewalk when Don was off it, striding toward the stupid ship-shaped entrance booth where the kid who'd made his life hell stood, wearing his stupid pirate hat. "I hear your boyfriend's leaving, and all it took was a phone call," Krepke sneered at him between customers as he saw Don coming.

Don didn't stop, picking up speed as he approached the window. With a leap, he jumped the desk and landed on Harmon. Harmon's hat went flying as Don drew back and plastered him in the nose with everything he had. Blood spattered everywhere as Don swung his fist back and smashed it into Harmon's stomach.

"Next time maybe you'll keep your fucking nose out of other people's business, you useless sack of shit! I'm one kid you're never going to bully again, do you hear me?" Don climbed back over the counter, ignoring the stares and openmouthed gapes, and walked back toward his bike. Picking it up, he rode back toward his house without looking back.

The adrenaline lasted until he reached his driveway, and then he wanted to collapse. Don made it into the drive and managed to put his bike in the shed and lock it up before his legs nearly gave out. Climbing the steps to the door was hard, but he made it into the house before collapsing onto the sofa, his face in his hands.

"Honey, what happened? Are you hurt? There's blood on your shirt," his mother fussed, and Don shook his head.

"It's not mine," he choked out before he started to cry. "Jay's gone, Mom." Don couldn't contain his grief anymore. He knew that Jay was a mile away in his parent's beach house, but to Don he was gone and out of reach. "His parents are taking him back to Chicago tomorrow." He tried to say more, but he couldn't breathe enough to do it. He felt his mother sit down next to him, wrapping her arms around him.

"Jay will be back next year," she soothed, but all Don could do was shake his head.

"He'll never be back. They're taking him away because I loved him." The last of Don's control broke, and he clutched at her, burying his head in her shoulder, sobbing. "He's gone because I loved him and he loved me," Don managed to say as he felt tears streaming down his cheeks. He felt his mother holding him, rocking him slightly like she had when he was a child. "They're taking him away because he loved me."

"I know, honey, I know," she said softly into his ear. "It's hard to lose the people you love." He was about to ask her how she knew, and then he remembered the way she'd lost his dad. To Don, his dad was a faint memory, but she must have felt the loss with the intensity that he was feeling the forced separation from Jay. "Why don't you take a minute and tell me what happened," she said calmly, still hugging him. Don tried, but couldn't for a long time. His mom was patient and continued comforting him for as long as he needed. Then, once he was ready to talk, he wasn't sure how to begin. Was he ready to tell her? Then he realized what she'd said. When he looked at her questioningly, she nodded slowly.

"How did you know?" Don asked, wiping his eyes as he sat up.

"I didn't for a while, but it was a number of things. I think the one that told me for sure was the way you looked at each other when you were together. There was something warm and special, like you knew each other inside and out." His mother fished into her pocket and pulled out a tissue. "It reminded me of the way your father looked at me." She wiped her eyes with the tissue. "So what happened?"

"Krepke saw us this afternoon. We were happy and we thought we were alone, and I kissed him. Krepke told Jay's parents, and his dad went ballistic. I heard him on the phone yelling at Jay, and when I went over there to try to see him, I saw Jay's computer broken in the yard. He must have sent me the last e-mail before his dad got to it." Don tried not to think about the fact that Jay was still there, close, and yet cut off from him. "He knew his dad would hate that he was gay, but…."

"You shouldn't have gone there," she said lightly.

"I had to try to see him." Don wiped his eyes again. "Mom, he looked so unhappy. They were mean to him, and I think his dad probably hit him." Don's insides clenched at the thought of anyone hurting Jay. "I saw him in his bedroom window, and he

76

must have known I was out there because he called for me, but his dad must have heard and made him close the window." Tears threatened once again, but Don held them back this time. "I know there's nothing I can do, but I miss him already, and I know I'll never see him again. His dad will see to that, I'm sure."

"You never know, honey. He may be mad now, but he could change his mind later." His mom was so practical about things.

"You aren't angry?" Don asked a bit surprised.

"Of course not. I was confused, and a little disappointed that you were gay, but I'm not angry. You're my son, and I've always said I'd love you no matter what, and I meant that." Don hugged her and began to cry again. "What's this for?"

"Jay told me today he wished you were his mother. We sort of fought about it because I didn't think he appreciated what he had, and maybe he was right. Maybe I am the lucky one, because I have you." Don continued holding her, and a few times he thought he heard his mother sniffle. When Don released her, she looked him over, examining his shirt.

"Where did the blood come from?" she asked.

Don looked at his shoes. "I punched Krepke in the nose." Don tried not to let it show, but that was the one thing he was proud of. "I was so angry I wasn't thinking, and I beat the crap out of him for telling Jay's folks. He's a huge bully, and he's been picking on me for years," Don told her in a rush. "I couldn't take it anymore, and when he taunted me about calling Jay's father, I punched him." Don couldn't help the smile that followed. "You should have seen it, Mom. He was wearing that stupid pirate hat and everything."

The phone rang, and his mother got up to get it while Don reached for a tissue off the coffee table. "Yes," he heard his mother say. "A broken nose—" She turned to Don with a scolding look. She listened for a while, and Don felt terrible.

"Well, it sounds to me as though he got what he deserved. Harmon's been a bully for years, and I can get half the school to back me up on that. You reap what you sow." She listened for a few more minutes, and Don wondered what was going to happen. "You go right ahead, but remember, I know what you were like at that age, and you were no angel, either. I suggest you teach that boy of yours some manners. He's a bully and he got what he deserved, and I can make it so everyone in town knows it." A minute later, she hung up the phone. "You know you shouldn't be punching anyone," she told Don with a scowl that she held for a second before smiling. "But there are exceptions, and this was one of them." She turned away. Don just felt wrung out.

"I'm gonna go to my room," he told her. He wanted to check his e-mail again. Getting up, he went into the room and switched the phone line to his modem. When it connected, he logged on and got a message that the account had been closed. He tried again and got the same thing. Then he remembered—Jay had given him that account to use, but now it was gone. Another link between them had been severed. Don closed his eyes and kept another wave of grief at bay. He'd been hoping that once Jay was back at school he would try to get in touch, but that was gone too now. At least Jay knew his phone number.

"Something came for you today," his mother said from the kitchen, and he heard her footsteps as she came into his room. "I'm glad you've been applying to colleges."

"I didn't apply anywhere," he said, taking the large envelope his mother handed him. It said it was from Virginia Tech, and he opened it, figuring it was some sort of junk mail.

"What does it say?"

"It's just a form letter," he told her as he read. "Wait—"

Dear Mr. Pottier,

78

We were very pleased to get your letter of inquiry and were very impressed by the game program you sent along with it. Enclosed you will find an application to Virginia Tech along with instructions regarding the application process. When the time comes, I hope you will apply "early decision." Pending verification of the information contained in your inquiry, we believe we can offer you a full academic scholarship to attend Virginia Tech at that time. Please contact me directly once you have provided the required details. I look forward to hearing from you and would be very pleased to have you call yourself a Hokie.

Don looked at his mother. "Did you send them anything?" She shook her head. "Because I didn't." Don reread the letter, and then pulled out the other forms, looking them over, but they appeared standard and shed no light on any of this.

"Then who did?" she asked, and Don looked toward the computer that sat on his desk and then back to his mother. And only one name came to mind.

"It must have been Jay," Don answered. "This would be the kind of thing he'd do. He's been after me to apply to schools since the beginning of the summer, but I knew we couldn't afford it." Don picked up the letter, still finding it hard to believe.

"I'll help you with the forms, and we'll get them mailed back as soon as they'll accept them," his mother told him as he began looking through the papers.

"But what about you? Aren't you going to need me?"

His mother set the pages she'd been holding on the stack. "Don't you worry; I'll be fine." Her eyes hardened as she spoke. "You need to get an education and off this island. I'll do whatever it takes to make sure you have a better life than I did." She walked around the bed and sat on the edge as Don watched her closely. "You have an opportunity here that only comes along once in a lifetime, and I won't allow you to squander it because of me or anyone else. I want you to go, and I want you to make me proud." Don moved and sat next to her.

"But what…." So much had happened in the last few hours that Don was having trouble thinking clearly.

"No buts, honey. This is right for you." She touched Don's cheek lightly. "If you love Jay like you say you do, and if he did this to help you, then you need to do this." Without another word, his mother stood up and left the room, closing the door behind her.

Don stared after her for a few seconds as the magnitude of what had happened sank in. Not only was he being offered the chance to go to college, but Jay had proven to him how much he loved him. More than anything in the world, he wanted to march over there and tell him, his parents be damned. Instead, he took the letter, folding it neatly, and placed it in the wooden box on his desk.

DAY 4

FIVE YEARS LATER
CHINCOTEAGUE ISLAND, VA

DONALD woke up in a hotel room outside Newport News and peered at the clock next to the bed. Not that he'd slept much, but the night before he'd been falling asleep behind the wheel of his car, so he'd found a hotel and tried to get some sleep. The last week had been sheer hell, but he'd made it through his last week of final exams, and he was heading home. But this was not the way he'd expected to be making the trip. Yesterday he'd had everything packed and ready, and he'd finished his last exam at five o'clock on sheer adrenaline and willpower. Then he'd left campus for what he expected would be the last time and had gotten within two hours of home before the last of his energy had given out. He'd been running on very little sleep and a whole lot of worry for weeks, and two days ago he'd received the call he'd been dreading for weeks, telling him that his mother had passed away from cancer.

When he'd been home to see her during his last break, she'd made him promise, three times, that no matter what he would finish school, and that if anything happened to her, he'd make sure to take his exams. "I know it won't be long now, Donny," she'd told him, and she'd been right. He'd been hoping to make it home one last time to see her, but she wouldn't hear of it. "Your finishing school is the most important thing. It's what I want more than anything else." And he was a good son, and he'd done what she wanted. Together they'd made all her final arrangements, so all he needed to do now was get home, because the service was being held late this afternoon. Thankfully, he only had two hours to go, and if he hurried, he'd be there by nine in the morning. Donald got out of bed, shaved, cleaned up, and jumped in the shower. After dressing and putting everything in the car, he got himself on the road before seven o'clock.

He'd made this trip a number of times over the past four years, but not nearly as often as he'd have liked. Being on the exact opposite end of the state, with four hundred miles between him and home, had made it difficult to visit, but he had gone whenever he could. For his last year of high school and his first three years of college, his mother's health had been good. The doctors had kept a close eye on her and were even about to declare her cancer-free. But a year ago, she'd told him she was feeling tired a lot, and after running tests, they'd found another tumor, a small one, on her kidney that they removed and treated, but unfortunately that was only the beginning. She'd fought it all the way up until about three months ago, when she didn't have the energy to fight anymore, and had forbidden any more treatments. At the time, he'd offered to take the semester off and come home, but she had been adamant that he finish school. She had been proud of him for getting into Virginia Tech, and she'd encouraged him the entire way through. She'd told him six months ago that her dream was to see him graduate. Donald teared up and wiped his eyes as he thought that now she wouldn't be there with him when he did. His mother had supported everything he'd done for years, to her own detriment, he knew that, but he could never argue with her. When he'd tried the last time he'd seen her, she'd given him that same "I'm your mother and I know best" look she always had that he could never argue with. Now, making this trip, he wondered if he'd done the right thing, but he could hear his mother's voice telling him how proud she was.

Donald's stomach rumbled when he was outside of Norfolk, and he made a run through a drive-through, eating the food as he drove but tasting none of it. Turning north, he passed over and through the Chesapeake Bay Bridge-Tunnel and then headed up the peninsula. As he got closer, he started to feel like he was going back in time, and when he turned off the main highway onto the road to the island, everything looked the same as it always had.

A while later, he crossed the tidal flats, with their marsh grasses that seemed to go on forever, dotted with cranes, herons, and egrets. These were views he'd seen all his life, but now they seemed a bit foreign. He'd always called the island home, but with his mother gone, it felt different, like his last tie to the place where he'd grown up and to his childhood was now gone. Donald crossed the bridge and passed into town. Stopping at the traffic signal, he looked around. The theater and businesses looked the same—the only thing that had changed was the name of the film. Making the turn, Donald drove down the business district before turning onto the main road across the island. He passed Mr. Whippy, not yet open for business, and then Pirate Miniature Golf, remembering the day he'd finally stood up for himself, the day he'd lost Jay. It had been five years, and Donald wondered why it still hurt sometimes. Right now he figured he was being extra emotional and tried to push the memory aside as he made the turn toward home, or what had been home.

Donald passed homes that hadn't changed, either, before pulling into the driveway and parking next to the house. He got out, stopped at the base of the steps and looked around him.

"Donny," he heard, and turned to see Mrs. Klingbeil, their neighbor and landlord, walking with her cane across the grass.

Before he knew it, she had him in a hug that reminded him a bit of his mother. "I'm so sorry," she said softly.

"Thank you," Donald told her, returning the hug.

"The house is the same. I cleaned it a little for you, but left everything." She wiped her eyes. "Your mother was so proud of you. When I visited her last week, the little she said was about you." Don didn't know what to say. His emotions were so close to the surface that he simply nodded.

"Thank you," he finally said with a swallow, looking toward the back door of the house he'd grown up in. "I'll be here for a few days, and I should be able to clean out the house for you."

She took his hand, patting it lightly. "You don't need to worry about that. Take everything you want. Your mother asked me months ago to settle things here for you if you needed it."

Donald didn't know what to say. "Thank you so much," he said softly.

"It's no problem. Your mother and I were friends for years. I watched you grow up here, remember?" She turned and slowly climbed the stairs, unlocking the door for him. Donald had his key, but Mrs. Klingbeil had always been helpful, and right now, he was grateful for her kindness.

The house looked the same as he stepped inside, sort of like a bit of a time capsule now. Much of the furniture was what had always been there, although there was a new chair and a few other things he'd bought his mother with the money he'd earned from his part-time and summer jobs. He doubted there was much he wanted to keep, but he wandered around the small house, seeing the shabby furniture and mismatched, well, everything. But it had always been home, and Donald realized that was because his mother had made it that way. Without her, everything felt empty and old. As he wandered through the rooms, he heard

Mrs. Klingbeil in the kitchen, and when he returned, she had made two mugs of coffee and they sat at the table.

"Your mother made me promise to tell you something when I saw you," Mrs. Klingbeil told him before taking a sip from her mug. "She said that I was to make sure you didn't feel guilty about anything. She was so proud of you, and your finishing school became the one thing she wanted more than anything else."

Donald took a sip from the mug before setting it back on the table. "They would have let me take a semester off, and I could have gone back next year. I tried to tell her...." Don lifted the mug again to cover the wave of emotion that once again threatened the thin veneer of control he was maintaining.

"You were all she cared about." Mrs. Klingbeil took his hand. "She wanted you to have a better life. That's why she worked so hard all those years, and that's why she wouldn't let you come back." Mrs. Klingbeil reached for a napkin from the holder in the center of the table, the same one he'd made in Boy Scouts years ago, and dabbed her eyes. "She wanted you to have a chance to be happy."

"But I could have spent the last few months with her," Donald countered, standing up and looking around the kitchen.

"Donny, for the last few months, your mother wasn't herself most of the time. She didn't remember things, and she couldn't control anything around her. She didn't want you to see that." Mrs. Klingbeil stood up, using her cane to walk to the door. "Remember your mother the way she was, because that's what she would have wanted, you know that. Guilt is a useless emotion, because we can't change anything, and I, for one, firmly believe that everything happens for a reason." She opened the door and stepped outside. "If you need anything, just stop over or call." The door closed behind her, and Donald stared down at the cup of coffee.

Somehow Donald doubted that his mother getting cancer had happened for a reason, other than bad luck and the fact that she'd worked all those years in a building as smoky as a chimney, but he didn't say that. Donald finished his coffee and then used the phone to make a few calls about flowers and things for the funeral. The visitation was at eleven and the funeral early that afternoon. He hadn't seen any reason to wait. His mother had already been cremated, as she'd requested, so Donald was having the simple service she'd helped plan.

As he walked to what had been his bedroom, Donald stopped at the door. Most things looked the same. His old computer sat at his old desk, silent and dark. After he'd gotten a new one a few years ago, he hadn't had the heart to throw that one away, so he'd brought it home and put it in the same place it had occupied when he and Jay had played *Catching Crabs* on it. Stepping closer, he saw the wooden box Jay had sent to him after a vacation with his family. Picking it up, he ran his hand over the carving on top before opening it. Inside were some of the mementos and bits of junk his adolescent self had once thought important. He closed the lid and set the box next to the computer, making a small pile of things he wanted to take. Opening the closet door, he expected to find his old clothes, but it was largely empty. After taking another look around, he left the room before stopping at his mother's closed bedroom door. This was going to be the hard part, going through his mother's things to decide what bits and pieces of his mother's life would be kept and what would be given away, or…. Donald stopped himself from thinking about that. Turning the knob, he pushed open the door.

He could almost smell the perfume she wore as he stepped into the room. It was what she'd always wanted for Christmas. Looking at the dresser, he saw the partial bottle sitting with his mother's other things. Peering around the room, it seemed the same, if a little stale. His mother hadn't actually been in here in almost two months because she'd either been in the hospital or hospice care. He walked to the dresser, opened an old jewelry box, and found the few things that were precious to his mother: her engagement ring and other bits of jewelry that Donald's father had given her. He picked up the box, carried it out of the room, and placed it with the other things he wanted to take. There really wasn't much, and he just wasn't up for tearing through his mother's things right now. Checking his watch, he figured it was time to get ready to go to the church.

He left the house, got his bag from the trunk of the car and brought it back inside and to his room. After slipping out of his clothes, Donald grabbed his kit and used the bathroom to clean up and take a shower before dressing to leave.

It didn't take long to drive to the small church his mother had attended on the other side of town. Donald hadn't been there in years other than to go with his mother for Christmas services, but the young minister remembered him and shook his hand as he entered. "Your mother was a special lady," he told Donald, who nodded and thanked him, because he didn't know what else to do. "Come on inside," the minister added, and Donald followed him into the narthex, where a table had been set up with candles and the urn that held his mother's ashes. It was surrounded by flowers, tons of flowers.

"Where did these come from?" Donald asked as he began reading the cards.

"As I said, your mother was a special lady. After you went to school, she started a women's cancer survivors group, and they got together here once a week; still do as a matter of fact." He stood off to the side as Donald stared. "I'll give you a few minutes," he said quietly. "People should start arriving in fifteen minutes or so. Just relax and don't feel you need to talk if you aren't ready. Everyone understands." He smiled at him and then left Donald alone.

Donald moved around the area, looking at the flowers and even the small urn, but he really didn't feel anything. His mother wasn't there, he knew that, but it didn't stop him from missing her, and he found himself talking to her. "I miss you, Mom," he said softly, standing in front of the urn. "Nothing feels the same here without you," Donald said as he felt tears start to well once again. "I'm alone now. For as long as I can remember, it was just you and I, and now you're gone, and I'm alone." Donald felt his head bow forward as he finally let the tears come. He'd been holding them in for long enough that he couldn't stop them anymore. He knew it was okay to grieve, and he also knew he'd do that for a while. While his mother's death was not unexpected, what was getting to him were the feelings of loneliness.

Wiping his eyes, he actually felt better as he walked to the restroom. After splashing a bit of cool water on his face, he used a paper towel to dry himself and then returned to the narthex as the first people began to arrive.

Donald greeted everyone as they came in and talked to the people he'd known and who had known him since he was a child. Some of the ladies brought in coffee and a donut to settle his stomach before the service. They told him stories about his mother that Donald had never heard. Some of them even had him laughing, and it felt good to laugh, especially when he remembered her.

"If you'd all like to take your places, we'll begin the service," the minister said.

His mother's urn and the flowers had already been carried into the sanctuary. The others filed in, and Donald was about to take his place when he saw the church door open. He stopped for a second, and then Jay took his first step into the church.

"Donny, is that you?"

Memories flooded through him as the sound of that familiar voice triggered a flood of sights and sounds. "Jay?" he asked tentatively as the man walked in from out of the glare of the sun and Donald saw him clearly. He'd filled out a lot and actually seemed taller, but his eyes had the same mischief in them.

"How are you, Donny?" Before he could answer, Jay hugged him tight, and the control Donald had tried to muster for the past two hours broke. He could hardly believe Jay was here. He hadn't seen or heard from him since that day five years earlier, when Jay's father had taken him away.

"I'm okay. How are you?" he asked, because it seemed like the thing to say and because he had no idea what else to ask. He was just floored and could barely comprehend that Jay was there.

"I think they're starting. You should take your seat, and I promise I'll be here after the service." Jay gave him a smile, one that he remembered well, and Donald nodded before walking to the front of the church and taking his seat so the service could begin.

It was simple and without a great deal of formality. The minister spoke about Don's mother and offered a prayer. Then he invited members of the congregation to come forward and say a few words. People stood and told brief stories or said kind words. But when Jay came forward, Donald's breath caught in his throat, and he reached for the tissue he'd shoved in his pocket.

"I remember the first night I met Mrs. Pottier. I was with Donny, and he and I were going crabbing, but she insisted we eat before we left. Now, being a growing boy, I was always hungry. That night she fed me the best crab cakes I have ever eaten." Jay stopped speaking for a moment, and Donald heard soft murmurs of assent, which he knew would have made his mother proud. "What I didn't realize right away was that she was giving me her dinner. There wasn't a lot of food, but she made sure Donny and I had a plate first." Jay, who'd been scanning the crowd as he talked, turned his eyes to Don. "She was always like that, putting others before herself, taking care of the people who mattered to her." Jay's expression shifted slightly. "I knew Mrs. Pottier when I was a teenager, and at the time, I once told Don that I was jealous of him because...." Donald heard a slight hitch in Jay's voice. "... because of his mother. She didn't have much as far as material possessions, but she took what she had, infused it with love, and created something wonderful. I grew up in a home where I had every material possession, but what I wanted was what Donny had. I wanted a mother like Mrs. Pottier, and to be honest, I still do." Jay stepped down and walked back to his seat as Donny wiped his eyes once again.

Others came forward to say a few words, and then it was his turn. Donald had known that he would be expected to say something, and he'd tried to think of what he wanted to say. As he stood up, he still hadn't figured out what he was going to say, but by the time he took those last steps to the front of the church, he knew.

"My mother loved me; of that I have no doubt whatsoever. She was there when I learned how to ride a bike and she was there, taking her life in her hands, helping me learn to drive a car. She was also there when I got a letter a number of years ago that I was being offered a scholarship to Virginia Tech. At the time, she was fighting the first round of cancer, and she told me that all she wanted was for me to have a better life than she had. At the time, I didn't completely understand things, but I think I do now. You see, when she told me that, I had everything, because I still had her." Donald felt the lump in his throat that had dissipated for a while begin to form again. "Mom, I never had any doubt that I was loved." He decided to speak directly to her. "You showed me that every day, and you never stopped giving of yourself. I know you were proud of me, but I'm also proud of you. Mom, you were the mother every boy dreams of, because you gave me something I now realize is precious and very rare: unconditional love. There were never any strings attached to your affection, and I will carry that with me for the rest of my life." Tears ran down his cheeks, and Donald did nothing to stop them. He couldn't have if he'd tried, but he kept his voice clear so he could finish. "More than anything, I hope you're at peace, free from pain. You used to tell me after Dad died that he was with the angels. Well, you were always one of them, so I hope you have a fluffy cloud up there to look down from and help take care of us." Donald couldn't continue. His throat ached, so he simply ended with, "I love you, Mom, and I always will," before sitting back in his seat.

No one moved, and Donald heard sniffles throughout the church. He wiped his own eyes as the minister said some final words that Don didn't really hear. Then the minister dismissed everyone with a prayer, and Don heard the others begin to leave, but he stayed where he was. A few people walked up to him, saying some last kind words or simply touching his hand in a show of sympathy before quietly leaving the church.

Finally, Donald stood up and walked through the empty sanctuary to the back of the church, where some of the women mourners had gathered. Tables had been set up, and a lunch was being served by the women of the church. Mrs. Klingbeil told him to go through the line, and then she escorted him to his place. He sat down and was surprised to see Jay sitting across from him. Donald took a deep breath to try to clear the cobwebs. "How have you been, Jay?"

"Good," he answered. "I'm about to graduate premed from the University of Chicago. How are you?"

"I graduate from Virginia Tech next week, and I have a job waiting for me with Rockwell. I'll be working in computer design in their office outside Richmond," Donald explained, and he saw Jay break into a smile as he chewed a bite of ham.

"You got the scholarship?" Jay asked.

"I did, and I know it was because of you," Donald said, but Jay shook his head.

"Any scholarships you got were because of you. All I did was bring you to their attention. Everything that happened was because of the work you did and your talent." Jay took a drink from his coffee cup. "Are you still developing video games?" Jay asked with excitement in his voice.

"Sometimes. Lately I've been busy finishing the work for my degree, and once I start my new job in a few weeks, I'll be busy then, but I have a few ideas I've been mulling over," Donald explained. They didn't have a chance to talk much more, and Jay stepped back because people started coming over, wishing Don well and offering their sympathies throughout the rest of the lunch. Donald ate a little, but mostly he talked with people and accepted their good wishes. Once the lunch was over, people continued saying goodbye and wishing him well, some sharing a final story about his mother. By the time he was alone with the minister, Donald found he felt better and less sad. His mother had been loved and cared for by the people on the island.

"What would you like to do with the flowers?" the minister asked as Donald was getting ready to leave. "We can deliver them to the nursing home and shut-ins if you like."

"That would be perfect," he said before lifting one of the small planters to take with him. He took the urn as well, not yet knowing what he was going to do with the ashes. It was the one thing they had never discussed, and Don wasn't ready to make that decision quite yet. He thanked the minister and left the church feeling a bit better than he had a few hours earlier. He was pleasantly surprised to see Jay standing out front waiting for him.

After Jay's folks had taken him away, Donald had been sad, but over time, that sadness had turned to anger and resentment because Jay had never tried to get in touch with him. Now even those feelings had mellowed as well. "Do you need some help?" Jay asked, taking the planter.

"Thank you," Donald said as he opened the car door. He carefully placed the urn so it wouldn't fall and then set the planter on the floor. "I appreciate it."

"Would it be okay to go somewhere and talk?" Jay asked.

"Sure. Would you like to come back to the house for a while?" Jay nodded. "Do you remember how to get there?"

"Not really. I haven't been back here since…." Jay's voice trailed off, and Donald knew exactly what Jay was referring to.

"You can follow me; it isn't very far," Donald said before getting into his car. He waited a minute and saw a newer BMW sedan pull up to the entrance of the church parking lot. He pulled out and waited as Jay fell in behind him before driving the short distance to the house he and his mother had shared. Donald parked in the drive, got out, and retrieved the urn and flowers before climbing the steps to the back door. Carrying the plant, Jay followed behind and joined him inside.

"It looks almost the same," Jay commented as he set the plant on the table. Donald walked into the living room and gently placed the urn on the coffee table. He'd been dying to ask Jay all kinds of questions since he'd first seen him, but he'd held back. Sitting down, Donald watched as his first love sat in the chair across from him. "You have to be wondering what happened."

"I know part of it," Donald said, a bit relieved that he hadn't had to ask.

"Krepke called my father," Jay explained.

"I know. He taunted me about it, and I beat the shit out of him for that." Donald grinned, remembering that incident. It was the only time he'd ever used force on another person, but it had felt good to stand up for himself, and it had given him strength to know he could defend himself.

"You did?" Jay smirked.

"Yeah, I broke his nose," Donald answered, and he saw Jay smile. "I know your dad broke your computer, I saw the pieces against the tree."

Jay's eyes widened. "So you *were* outside the beach house that night."

Donald nodded slowly. "I heard you calling for me, but couldn't answer without your folks hearing, and I didn't want to make things worse for you. I know your dad wouldn't let you call, and I know about the computer, but I guess I always wondered why you never tried to contact me later." Donald felt some of the old hurt begin to surface.

"I thought about it. I wanted to call so many times, but my father kept close tabs on me. He had one of his assistants look over my phone bills, and I found out that he would call any number he didn't know to see who they were. When I went back to school, he made sure I had limited Internet access, and he canceled my e-mail account," Jay said, and Donald nodded. That he knew. "He also threatened to cut me off if I ever saw or talked to you again. Once I got to college, I tried looking you up a few times. I even found you at Virginia Tech, but by then, I…." Jay took a deep breath. "I figured you had moved on and would probably be better off going on with your life. Goodness knows, you didn't need me and my problems." Donald wondered what could be so bad. "My dad promised that he'd pay for college and even medical school, but…."

"Let me guess: you have to be a good boy or he'll stop paying," Donald said, and Jay nodded.

"Exactly," Jay admitted and looked at the floor.

Donald's first reaction was to wonder what had happened to the boy he knew—the one who'd taken on two bullies at once to save him and wasn't afraid of anyone. "Does he know you're here?" Donald asked.

Jay shook his head. "He thinks I'm visiting friends in Ocean City. I haven't spoken about you to anyone, least of all him, in so long, he can't suspect. I've been a good student, and he hasn't heard anything that would make him think I'm not where I'm supposed to be. My friends really are in Ocean City, and they know where I am and why. Renee is amazing. My dad thinks she's my girlfriend, and her family thinks I'm her boyfriend, but she's actually a lesbian and isn't ready to tell her folks. She and I have been roommates for the last year." Jay rolled his eyes. "My dad is so proud," he mocked. "How are things for you? Did you tell your mother?"

"Yes. I told her that night. I was heartbroken that you were leaving, and she told me she already knew. When I asked her how she knew, she said she'd seen it in the way we looked at one another. I had a hard time after you left." It still wasn't an easy subject for him to think about. "But Mom was there for me, and it was then I understood that her love wasn't conditional on anything I did. It was simply there, like a force of nature."

"That's what I always wanted, because I found out my parents' love was conditional on many things, not least of which is behaving exactly how they want me to. At least that's how it is with my father. My mother is harder to understand because she doesn't talk much about how she feels about anything." Jay's expression darkened, and Donald could see the disappointment and hurt that simmered just under the surface, and their conversation ground to a halt for a few moments.

"Can I get you something to drink?" Donald asked to break the uncomfortable silence.

"No, thank you, I'm fine," Jay answered, and Donald settled back into his chair.

"How did you learn about the funeral?" Donald inquired.

Jay's expression shifted, and for a second Donald thought he was going to tell a joke, because his eyes glinted with a hint of mischief. "You'll never believe it, but I ran into, of all people, Harmon Krepke a few months ago, during spring break. I barely recognized him, but he remembered me. He actually apologized for what he'd done, and he told me about your mother. I wanted to visit her, but didn't dare, but I gave Harmon my phone number so he could keep me updated. It was a bit of a coincidence that I was planning to come out here when he called and told me she'd passed away and that the funeral was today. We came out a day early so I could be here."

"I'm glad you did," Donald told him. Seeing Jay again was nice, and it felt good to talk to him. He'd always wondered what had happened to Jay and where he was. "I know Mom would have been happy you came."

"Donny, I came because I knew it would probably be my only chance to see you. I knew you'd be here, and I took the chance that you'd actually talk to me."

"Of course I'd talk to you," Donald said with a smile. "What happened wasn't your fault. It was mine. If I had been more careful, we wouldn't have been found out. But even then it would have been just a matter of time. We might have had one more summer and then we would have had to go our separate ways." But knowing that hadn't made the separation any easier or less painful.

"I hated my parents for what they did. In some ways I still do."

"I hated them too. I used to think about creative ways I'd get even when they came back. I used to ride out there every day just to convince myself that you were truly gone. I knew you were never coming back when I saw a for-sale sign on the house a week after you left. I think it was then that I made myself give up any hope of seeing you again."

Jay looked miserable for just a moment, and then the look passed.

"How long can you stay?" Donald asked.

"I should probably be back in Ocean City this evening," Jay answered, and Donald smiled. "Why?"

"You wanna drown some chicken necks for old times' sake?" As soon as he said the words, they sounded stupid, but Jay grinned and nodded. "I still have the supplies in the shed. I need to change first, though."

"No problem. I brought some jeans with me." Jay stood up. "I'll go get them from the car." Jay was out the door in a hurry, and Donald heard quick treads on the stairs. Going to his room, he pulled off his clothes and stepped into an old pair of jeans.

"You're even more beautiful now than you were then," Jay said, and Donald turned to see Jay standing in the open bedroom doorway. Donald felt a bit self-conscious with Jay looking intently at him with his shirt off. Part of him wanted to walk to Jay and kiss him hard, to let the past five years melt away. The look on Jay's face was just like Donald remembered, heated, passionate, and if he wasn't mistaken, he thought Jay might still love him. God knew the lingering feelings he'd harbored for the past half decade would easily rekindle to love if he allowed them. Instead, Donald picked up his shirt and pulled it over his head.

"I'll let you change," Donald said, motioning for Jay to use the room. On his way out, Donald closed the door and then he waited in the living room for Jay to get ready. Part of him—okay, a huge, screaming part of him—wanted to take Jay up on his silent offer and spend the day lost in his arms once again. But he couldn't do that to himself or his heart. Donald closed his eyes, and he could almost feel the way Jay's arms would encircle him, how Jay's lips would taste, and even how Jay's stronger, more muscular body would feel under his hands. His heart yearned to be with him one more time, but his head kept him at bay. Jay had one day here, and then he was going to leave. Even if he could stay a little longer, there was little point in getting involved again. Donald was set to move to Richmond so he could start his new job. No, he couldn't go back, no matter how much he wanted to. "I'll be out back in the shed," Donald called through the door before leaving the house and walking down the steps, enjoying the May warmth as he strode across the grass. Donald unlocked the shed and pulled open the doors. No one had been in it in quite a while, but everything was still there: his old bike, the nets, crab cages, even the mondo ball of string he always used. Pulling out a net and one of the cages, he set them on the grass along with the string and was about to close the door when he heard Jay's steps on the stairs.

"You kept everything," Jay said, hurrying up next to him. "Say, isn't that my net?"

"Yeah," Donald admitted. "When I saw the for-sale sign at your place, I broke into the storage room under the house and took the net and crab cage. I knew your dad wouldn't take them along, and I wanted them." They'd used them the last time he and Jay had been together. "I know it seems dumb now, but at the time I was hurting, and I hung on to everything that had anything to do with you." Donald closed the shed door. "Let's get going." He needed to change the subject.

They loaded the supplies in the back of Jay's car, since he was parked nearest the street. Donald navigated Jay to the grocery store, and they bought some bait. The man behind the counter wasn't anyone Donald recognized, so they didn't talk or linger, and once the chicken necks were packaged, they paid for them and left. "Does it seem strange to be back?" Jay asked him, and Donald had to admit that it did.

"I've been here to see Mom a number of times over the last five years, but once I went away to school, I could get better summer jobs elsewhere, so I worked there instead of spending summers here. In that short time, businesses have opened and closed, and many of the faces have changed. Some things will always be the same, but...." Donald paused for a few seconds. "I'm not sure it feels like home here anymore."

They got in the car and rode out to Mr. Winters's place. "Are you sure it's okay to be here?" Jay asked as they parked and got out of the car.

"Sure. I stop and see Mr. Winters every time I come back. He doesn't get around so well anymore, but he'll be out on his deck to say hello. He'll probably talk our ears off, since he doesn't get many visitors," Donald explained as they got their things out of the trunk, and they walked to the wooden dock that ran along the metal seawall. They set up their things and attached the chicken to the strings before dangling them in the water. Sure enough, Donald heard the glass doors slide open above them.

"Don, is that you?" Mr. Winters asked from above them.

"Sure is," he called back. "You remember Jason Greene. His family used to have the place up the street." As Donald expected, Mr. Winters talked their ears off for a while, asking about everything until the chill got to him and he headed back inside. "Go ahead and check the lines. I want to make sure the cage is secure for anything we get," Don said, and thankfully it was, because Jay hauled in two crabs in rapid succession, with more following behind.

"Have you done this much?" Jay asked while they sat in the sun, waiting to check the lines again.

"Nope. I went crabbing when my mother asked me to, but it was never much fun after...." Donald drifted to silence with a shrug. "A lot of things changed for me after you left. I worked more on the computer, and Mom said I was quieter and more withdrawn. I still worked at Mr. Whippy through high school, but other than that I didn't get out much."

"I saw the old computer in your room," Jay said, and Donald nodded. "Things changed a lot for me too. I didn't speak to either of my parents willingly until I went back to school. I ignored them as best I could, and they ignored me. You had told me once to give them a chance, but after what they did, I never could. We barely speak now unless my dad wants something. I know my dad is having an affair with his office assistant, and I think Mom is screwing one of the men at her spa. They're both so messed up, it's ridiculous," Jay said venomously.

"Then why do you let them run your life? You're an adult and you can earn your own money. Why do you let them control you?" Donald was convinced the Jay he'd first known and the Jay he'd fallen in love with wouldn't have done that. Something had changed in Jay, and he wasn't sure what it was, or even if Jay knew or realized it.

"I want to go to medical school, which costs a fortune, and after that I want to specialize, and that costs even more. Dad says he'll take me into his practice, but I have no intention of spending my life doing boob jobs, face-lifts, and penis enlargements, or liposuctioning the fat out of housewives with nothing better do with their husband's money." Jay got this wicked look on his face as Donald began to laugh. "I want to make a difference, and if I can get my dad to pay for most of what I need, so be it. He may have taken away what I loved most, but I'm going to make him pay as much as I possibly can for it." The venom in Jay's eyes was more than a little unsettling, and Donald was sorry he'd brought it up.

"Well, here you don't have to worry about any of that. All we need to do right now is keep the crabs from stealing our bait." Donald netted first one crab and then another. "If we get enough, I have my mother's recipe for crab cakes."

Jay smiled and made happy noises. "I haven't had a crab cake since the last time I was on the island. In fact, I think the last one I had was one of your mom's." Jay lapsed into silence, and they ended up staring at each other. "I'm sorry."

"What for?"

"Everything," Jay responded quickly. "I feel like everything is my fault. I should have moved heaven and earth to contact you and let you know that I was okay. We could have communicated over the years, even if it was just through letters. We could have…."

Donald lightly touched Jay's arm. "It's okay, and it wasn't your fault. What's done is done, and we can't change that." Donald checked the lines and then scooped out a crab that he put into the cage before sinking it back into the water. "Someone wise told me that guilt is a wasted emotion, and I think she was right. We've both been carrying around a lot of guilt and pain over what happened almost five years ago." Donald sat back down, looking into Jay's eyes. "Do I wish it hadn't happened? God, yes. I thought my heart had been torn out when you left and that your dad was taking you away because I loved you and because you loved me. I know now that your dad did it because he's the world's biggest bigoted asshole."

"You thought all this was because I loved you?" Jay asked, and Donald felt the almost forgotten feel of Jay's hand on his cheek. "Well, in a way you were probably right. My dad can't stand anything that's different from what he wants or expects, and me falling in love with you was something he couldn't and didn't understand." Jay looked as though he was thinking, so Donald remained quiet, checking the lines. "I don't know what happened to my father, but he's always been vehemently against gay people, and it doesn't make sense to me. When he was a teenager, he marched in the South for civil rights, and now he's as closed off as anyone I know." Donald shrugged his shoulders. "I have to admit that I used to wonder about him, but now he isn't worth the energy." Jay checked the lines, scooping up another crab before adding it to the cage. "Do you think we have enough?"

"I think so," Donald said, and he began to pull in the lines, cutting off the bait and throwing it into the water before gathering up their things. Donald called up to Mr. Winters, saying goodbye. They carried everything to the car and then hurried back to the house.

Don got out the same large pot his mother had used for years, and then added the water and spices before placing the water on to boil. "Get the crabs out of the cage and start putting them in the pot," Donald told Jay, and they began filling the pot with crabs before putting on the lid. "I always hated this part. The crabs still being alive in the pot really gets to me." The sounds from inside the pot didn't last long, and Donald monitored the steaming of the crabs. Once they were done, he took them out, cooled them, and then together he and Jay cracked them open to get the meat.

It didn't take long to mix the crab, breadcrumbs, and other ingredients into the crab cake mixture. Then they formed them into cakes, and Donald began frying them in a little oil. "I'll get the plates," Jay said, and he opened the cupboard where Donald's mother kept the dishes. Soon they were sitting at the old table with two plates of crab cakes and half a case of beer.

"Perfect," Jay said.

Donald couldn't help chuckling. Jay had the same expression Donald remembered from that first night he'd come over for dinner. "Yes, it kind of is," Donald agreed, eating slowly because he was watching Jay. He still felt a bit like Jay was his, even though he knew that wasn't the case. But here in his mother's home, he felt like the five years hadn't happened, and when Jay leaned close to him, Donald automatically turned and met his lips. He didn't have to think—it just happened and it felt right. Donald returned the kiss, deepening it. Jay tasted just like he remembered, everything was like he remembered. "We shouldn't do this," he protested mildly.

"I know," Jay told him before kissing him deeper, sucking lightly on his tongue, and Donald moaned softly. He'd dreamed of this for five years, this and so much more. "This is our chance to have one more night together," Jay added breathlessly.

Donald knew Jay was right, but his heart couldn't allow that, and he pulled back. "I can't, Jay. I don't want just a night. If we do this, I know it will hurt when you have to leave." Donald picked up his plate and carried it to the counter. "I've never been able to stop my feelings for you. I've tried over the last five years. I've even had a few boyfriends, but I always drove them away because they weren't you." Donald knew he would probably be kicking himself later for this. "I can't do this for just one night, when I know you have to leave." He turned to face Jay, leaning against the counter. "It's been amazingly wonderful seeing you again, it really has." Donald stepped closer to Jay, taking his hand. "I want to be with you almost more than I want to breathe right now, but if we do this and then you leave, it'll feel like it did five years ago, and I don't know if I can go through that again."

He could hardly believe he was saying this. He had a chance to be with Jay again, maybe only once, but still. Donald stared at the face that had captured his imagination almost every night since the day Jay's parents had taken him away. Anonymous sex was something Donald wasn't a particular stranger to. He'd had his fair share of bar pickups and languid looks from across a crowded classroom. After all, he had been to college. The hookups had been fun but at the same time meaningless. "Jay," Donald said, trying to find the words, "I've had one-night-stands. Sex with someone I've known for a few hours and wave at when I see them around campus a few days later." Jay was nodding slowly, and Donald knew he understood. "You could never be one of those guys." Donald stepped closer, touching Jay's cheek, his stubble rough on his palm. "You're so much more than just one night."

"But it's all we have," Jay countered.

"No, it's not. We have the time we spent together and the love we shared. That will always be with us. You were my first love, Jay, probably my only love up to this point, because I've never been able to get you out of my system. I have to, though, I know that, and I also know I'm feeling really emotional because of the funeral and all, but I could fall back in love with you so easily…." Donald felt another lump form in his throat, and he choked it down. "Because I do love you, Jay, I really do."

"Maybe I should go," Jay said, standing up.

"You don't have to, unless the only thing you came here for was sex," Donald said a little more harshly than he intended.

Jay's expression hardened instantly. "You know that isn't true."

"I know," Donald conceded. "So how about we take a walk before you have to go." Donald didn't want Jay to leave. Having him here was like an unexpected gift and a chance he might never get again.

"That would be nice," Jay agreed, and Donald took care of the dishes and food before grabbing a light jacket. Almost without thinking about it, they ended up walking down the main tourist street past Pirate Miniature Golf. "Harmon's dad still owns the place," Jay said softly. "Say," Jay said, stopping. "Did I tell you that when I saw Krepke, he had a boyfriend?" Donald had to make sure he'd heard right, and he saw Jay smiling and nodding. "He said they hadn't been together long, but they seemed happy together."

"Well, I'll be," Donald sighed softly. "I guess that explains a lot about him."

They didn't talk a lot as they walked, and that was fine. Donald knew that in a few hours Jay would have to go and that would be that. Their walk took them past Mr. Whippy, and they went inside, each getting an ice cream cone, and Don had to remind himself he didn't need to take it to the employee entrance to eat it. Once they were done, they walked back toward the house. By the time they got there, it was getting dark, and Donald knew that Jay's time with him was up. "I need to get back to Ocean City," Jay said, as if he'd been reading Donald's thoughts.

"I know," he said, and he gave Jay a hug. "It was great to see you." Donald could feel a part of him ready to tug Jay into the house in spite of what he'd said earlier.

"I wouldn't have missed it," Jay whispered, and Donald felt warm hands on his cheeks as Jay angled his face toward his. "I'll always love you, Donny." Jay kissed him gently, and Donald closed his eyes, trying to commit everything to memory: the taste of Jay's lips, the way he felt under Donald's hands, even the small sound he made when the kiss ended. He knew he was being sentimental, but he figured he was allowed. "I'll be in touch this time, Donny, I promise. Give me your number, and I'll use a friend's phone if I have to." Donald stared into Jay's eyes, and he knew Jay would try, but he didn't have any delusions, and this was probably the last time they would see each other.

"Take care of yourself and find someone who loves you. You deserve to be happy," Donald told Jay with a smile. He knew it was a bit forced. "No matter what your father thinks or feels, you deserve to be loved; you always have."

"You too," Jay told him, but Donald heard regret in Jay's voice as he looked into his eyes. For a few seconds, Donald thought Jay had something else to say, but the expression passed and Jay's hands slipped away from his cheeks, and Jay stepped back before opening the car door and climbing inside. Donald stood in the drive and watched as Jay pulled out of the drive and drove away, waving a silent goodbye. Once he was gone and the taillights had faded, Donald climbed the stairs, going back in the house.

He put away the dishes and cleaned up the kitchen. Not that it really mattered now. When he was done, Donald sat in the living room but didn't turn on the television like he'd intended to. Instead, he stared at the urn on the coffee table. He thought about hanging onto his mother's ashes until he could decide what to do with them, but he knew what had to be done. Picking up the urn, he left the house and carried it to the car. Before he could have second thoughts, he drove to town and parked near the bridge to the island. Getting out, he picked up the urn and began walking onto the bridge.

He walked past the drawbridge keeper's control box, and the man inside looked out at him. Donald didn't think he could speak without bursting into tears, but he saw the man nod, and then he stepped onto the bridge, walking toward the center.

The breeze was blowing out to sea, which was perfect. Donald could hear it and feel it as he stood in the center of the bridge. "You carried a torch for Dad all those years because you loved him so much. I know now exactly how you felt. Dad had your heart all these years, and you weren't about to give it to anyone else." Donald looked out over the water and opened the lid on the urn. "We don't know exactly where Dad is, but he's somewhere out there, so I'm scattering you on the water in the hope that you'll somehow be able to find each other again. Goodbye, Mom, I love you." Slowly, Donald tipped the urn and the ashes floated out of the container, the breeze carrying them away and out toward the sea.

Donald stood for a minute and watched as the gray dust settled on the water as the setting sun lit up the waves. Turning back toward the island, Donald saw the gates go up and cars began to cross once again. He hadn't even realized that they weren't there until he heard the first one rumble across the bridge. Reaching the control booth, Donald thanked the operator before walking to his car, placing the empty urn on the floor of the backseat. He wasn't sure where to go or what he wanted to do, so he ended up back at the house, sitting in the car in the driveway, thinking.

Eventually he got out and walked inside the house. He knew he had a lot of work to do to get the house cleaned out, but he didn't have the energy to start now. After getting undressed and cleaned up, Donald climbed into his bed and closed his eyes. The house seemed quiet and really empty. He was alone now, and he felt the feeling start to close in around him. He wanted to cry or scream at the unfairness of it all. He was twenty-two and his entire family was gone. Instead, Donald buried his head in the pillow and let what he vowed were the last tears come.

DAY 5

FIVE YEARS LATER
MILWAUKEE, WI

"HAPPY Birthday," Bobbi called from the desk next to Don as he set his bag down next to the cupcake she had obviously placed on his desk.

"Thank you," Donald said before giving her a hug. "But you remember that today I have an appointment with the doctor." Donald was finding it hard to be in a festive mood about turning twenty-seven.

"So why are you here?" she asked accusingly. "Not that I'm complaining, because then I couldn't give you this." She grinned and handed him a wrapped present. Donald hadn't gotten an official birthday gift in years. "Go ahead, open it," she said excitedly, and Donald obliged with a smile, tearing off the wrappings and opening the box. "I made them for you." Inside was a pair of hand-knitted mittens with a matching scarf and hat. "I sort of figured that since this is your first winter in the frozen north, you'll need something to keep you warm."

Donald gave her a hug. "Thank you. I needed something like this today, and this was really thoughtful." The worry he'd managed to keep at bay for days seemed to break over him all at once.

"So why are you here?" Bobbi asked as she sat down at her chair, already typing away. The woman was wonderful, with a brilliant mind, and she could also type and program while she was talking about something completely different. It was both amazing and infuriating.

"The doctor is only a mile away from here, and I need something to keep my mind off it," Donald replied, sitting down to get to work. Bobbi was the only person at the office that Donald had shared his suspicions and worries with. She was a big woman, with a heart of gold and a mind like a steel trap. Bobbi was a gifted programmer and systems designer who had the rare ability to see the big picture as well as the patience to drill down into the details when needed. She'd become one of Donald's best friends since he'd transferred from Richmond to Milwaukee six months earlier. She was, technically, Donald's boss, but they worked as a team, along with Randy, the third programmer, developing the code for a new flight simulation system for training military pilots.

Donald started his PC and logged in, making sure all his security protocols were functioning properly before starting to run their current program. "You know," Bobbi said from next to him, "I was thinking that we should tighten up the flight settings. I think there's too much play in the flight controls, and this needs to be as accurate as possible." Of all the people on the team, Bobbi was also the most experienced pilot.

"I was thinking we could make that configurable, so that instead of programming it, we could allow it to be set during testing. That way we're sure to get it just right. There has to be some difference between planes, even if it's small, and this will give the people running the test the ability to make the simulation feel like different physical planes," Don suggested.

"Perfect. Let's run that by the colonel when he comes in later this week," Bobbi agreed, and Donald looked to Randy, who was nodding as he continued working. Donald made an entry in the team's notes for the meeting and then continued with his coding.

Being busy helped pass the time, and Donald told Bobbi he was leaving before locking his workstation. He grabbed his coat and the mittens Bobbi had given him, smiling at her nervously before leaving their secured workroom and heading out of the building.

The frigid wind off Lake Michigan cut through his coat. Donald hurried to his car and started the engine to get some heat going before driving the short distance to the doctor's office, where he parked and hurried inside out of the cold. Donald was starting to wonder how he was going to make it through the entire winter. It was cold as hell, and they were only halfway through November.

The office was bright and quiet, with only one other person waiting. Donald gave his name to the receptionist and then sat down to wait. He'd filled out all the forms the last time he was here, so he didn't have anything to do but read a magazine article about the mating habits of penguins. "Mr. Pottier," the nurse said softly, and he got up, thankful for the interruption in his article reading, and followed her through into the office. "We're going to take some blood and things before the doctor sees you."

"Okay," Donald said with a shrug. He'd been through this a number of times already, so he knew exactly what to expect. She went through the procedure of tying the rubber thing on his arm and then cleaned his skin before sliding the needle in so easily he barely felt it. "You can do that anytime. The last time they took blood it hurt for two days." She gave him a smile and took his blood pressure and pulse. "I brought the samples they asked for," he told her before reaching into his bag and handing her the containers.

"Thank you. We're not sure if they'll be needed, but if they are, this should save a trip." She set everything on a tray. "Are you having any pain?"

"Do nerves that feel like they're ready to fry count?" Donald asked, and she chuckled. "Then no," he added.

"A sense of humor is important," she said, "and don't worry, Dr. Rivers is the best." She took a few minutes to enter everything into the computer. "It'll be just a few minutes." She left and Donald stared around the tiny room, thankful there were no anatomical pictures of bones and muscles on the walls. Those were just gross, and what were you supposed to do with them anyway? Study for medical school?

A few minutes later, the doctor opened the door and came in, leaving the door open behind him. "Morning, Donald. I have an intern who'll be working with me for the next few months, and I wanted to ask if it's okay if he sits in on your exam?"

"Of course," Donald answered, paying little attention as the other man stepped into the examination room.

"Donald, this is Jason Greene," Dr. Rivers said, and Donald stared, his mouth dropping open as Jay turned toward him. Neither of them spoke for a second. "Do you know each other?"

"Yes. Jay and I have known each other since we were teenagers," Donald answered.

Dr. Rivers turned to him seriously. "Is this going to be a problem? I can have him step out."

Donald couldn't keep the smile off his face. "No. There's no problem at all." Other than maybe the fact that his heart was racing a mile a minute. Jay looked amazing in dress pants and a crisp blue shirt, eyes sparkling and a smile on his handsome face—one that Donald was sure his other patients didn't get to see.

"Excellent," Dr. Rivers said, pulling Donald out of his thoughts and back to reality. "As we suspected and the biopsy confirmed, there's a small tumor on your left breast. It appears to be close to the surface. We suspect it hasn't been there long. What we'd like to do is schedule surgery to remove it so we can check it further. Then, if everything is as we suspect, we'll do a single round of chemotherapy."

Donald stared at the doctor, almost unable to believe what he was hearing. "You're saying I definitely have cancer?" He'd tried to prepare himself for the possibility, but he'd hoped it was nothing.

Dr. Rivers seemed surprised. "Didn't someone call you with the test results?"

"No. But I guess I sort of suspected when the nurse insisted on making an appointment." Donald thought he'd been prepared for this, but he wasn't.

"Doctor," Jay said softly, "Donny's mother died of cancer about five years ago."

Dr. Rivers looked at Jay, and then his gaze shifted back to Donald. "Yes, I see." Dr. Rivers pulled up a chair and sat in front of him. "Let's start at the beginning. The tumor itself is quite small, and it looks like we've caught it very early. Most people wouldn't think anything of a small bump under the skin and would wait months before bringing it to a doctor's attention."

"I only mentioned it during the company physical because the doctor happened to ask about lumps or anything unusual on my skin, because I'm so fair," Donald supplied, and Dr. Rivers nodded slowly.

"He did you a favor, because the earlier we catch something, the easier it is to treat. I'd like to schedule surgery next Tuesday. We can do it as a day surgery. You won't need to stay overnight and can go home by late morning. I'll have the nurse give you all the information you need." The doctor stood up and clapped him on the shoulder. "I see patients every day, and if all of them were as strong as you are, my job would be easy. I don't see any reason why you won't be just fine." Dr. Rivers walked to the door, and Donald seemed to sense some silent communication between him and Jay before he opened the door and left the room.

As soon as the door closed, Jay moved closer and Donald felt his friend's arms around him, his doctor demeanor gone in an instant. "It's so good to see you," Donald said. He had so many questions he wasn't sure where to start.

"I have to see other patients...."

"I know," Donald said, still a bit surprised to see Jay. They'd kept in touch for a little while after his mother's funeral, but with Jay in medical school and Donald's new job, they'd sort of lost touch again.

"Would you like to get together for dinner?" Jay asked.

"Sure," Donald answered. It had been a long time since he'd seen Jay, and it would be nice to catch up.

"There's a tapas place just down the street, Antonio's—we could meet there at seven," Jay offered, and Donald found himself nodding his agreement without thinking. "I have to go, but I can walk you out."

Donald gathered his things and followed Jay through to the lobby. He knew he was being naughty, but he couldn't help sneaking a peek at his butt as he walked. "Thank you, Jay," Donald said as he stood in front of the nurse, watching as Jay walked toward the back down the hallway.

"He is handsome, isn't he?" the nurse, Susan, said, and Donald blushed slightly as he turned to look at her. "It's okay. He plays for your team, I believe." She winked at him conspiratorially, and Donald let that tidbit soak in. "When he first arrived, all the women were gushing over him, but he hasn't noticed a one of them." She leaned closer to the counter. "When Mary went after him a little too strongly, he told her, and it spread through the office like wildfire. Of course, he's as nice as can be."

Something must have changed.

"He actually told her?" Donald asked, not really listening to the answer. Something had definitely changed, and that had Donald curious.

"He's really sweet, but kind of quiet," Susan told him.

"Jay and I are old friends," Donald explained as he heard Jay's voice from the back of the office, deep and rich, like hot chocolate, and that sent a chill through him even in the warmth of the office. "We knew each other as kids," he explained. It was definitely a small world.

Dr. Rivers stepped into the area, and Susan became all business, explaining the procedure at the hospital. "I've confirmed you for eight o'clock, so you need to be there at six thirty. They'll send you some information on what you can expect. The one thing you'll need is someone to drop you off and pick you up. They won't let you drive yourself home, and they will not allow you to take a cab either."

"Okay. Thank you," Donald said, and he took the paperwork, catching a brief glimpse of Jay before leaving the doctor's office and heading back to work.

"HOW'D it go?" Bobbi asked as soon as he returned to the office, and Donald looked around at the rest of the team and shook his head slowly. Her mouth formed into an "oh," and Donald got back to work. At lunch, she cornered him at a table in the cafeteria. "What did they say?"

"That I have breast cancer," Donald answered flatly. "He said we've caught it early, and I need to have outpatient surgery next week. After that, who knows." He was trying not to get too emotional, but it was becoming more and more difficult. "My mother died of cancer." That was what worried him more than anything else. Was this the start of what his mother had gone through?

"I think you told me once that she had lung cancer, right?" Bobbi asked, and Donald nodded. "What you have is very different. I know it doesn't mean much, but you're going to be fine. I know it." She leaned closer. "I had breast cancer about seven years ago. It was hard, but I got through it, and I've been healthy, and I take better care of myself because of it."

"I know I will be fine, but I can't keep away the fear. I didn't see everything that my mother went through because I was at school for a lot of it, but I saw the effects of the cancer and then the treatments. I don't want to go through that, not like she did."

"You won't," Bobbi said.

"How do you know? I don't. Mom got better and was doing really well for years after the initial treatments, and then the cancer returned and ate her alive," Donald said, pushing his lunch away from him because he wasn't hungry anymore.

"You take what life gives you and make the most of it." Bobbi always had these words of wisdom that sounded like platitudes, but she seemed to be able to deliver them when they needed to be said. "After the cancer, I decided to make the most of my life. Before the disease, I was shy and quiet." Donald grunted, because that was a bit of a stretch. "Yes, me. Afterwards, I started going out with friends, dating, and I met my husband. If the cancer comes back, then I know I made the most of what I was given." Bobbi ate a bit of cheese from her lunch. "I'm a survivor, and so are you."

Donald picked up his fork once again. "You're right. I am," Donald said with determination. "Now, you'll never guess who I'm having dinner with tonight."

"Who?" Bobbi looked like a wide-eyed teenager.

"The doctor's intern," Donald answered. He couldn't resist having a bit of fun. "I knew him when I was a kid, and you could have knocked me over with a feather when I saw him." Donald took a bite of his chicken Caesar.

"Is he cute?"

"He looks a lot like I remember him. Jay always had high cheekbones, bright eyes, and a butt you could bounce quarters off of." Donald laughed as Bobbi cackled. "He was my first love."

"Did he know how you felt?" Bobbi asked, and Donald told her the condensed version of his relationship with Jay.

"The last time I saw him was at my mother's funeral, and we spent the day together."

Bobbi stared at him. "You still care for him," she stated. "And don't bother denying it, because you get this mushy look in your eyes when you talk about him."

"I do not!" Donald cried, and then he lowered his voice as other people in the lunchroom turned to look at him.

"You do too," Bobbi countered, and Donald wondered if they were going to argue back and forth until they got into a slap fight or something. "I think it's sort of sweet. Do you think he still cares for you?"

"I don't know. We're having dinner tonight, and we'll probably talk about old times and then go our separate ways. Like

I said, I haven't seen him in five years, and that was just for part of a day. Before that we were seventeen years old."

"Yeah, but you were in love. I bet he was something?" Bobbi prompted, and Donald nearly missed the mischief in her eyes.

"Stop it. I see what you're doing," Donald protested, and Bobbi raised her eyebrows expectantly. "He was," Donald admitted with a chuckle. "The first day he spoke to me he saved me from the town bullies," Donald said, and he leaned closer to Bobbi as if he were going to share a secret. "And he kissed me that night. We were sixteen and instantly inseparable."

"See, you're all mushy."

"I know," he began with a sigh. "There's something about Jay that always gets me this way." Donald sighed as he continued his trip down memory lane. "You know, I'm here working with you because of him. He had an extra computer, and that first summer, he gave it to me when he left. I wrote my first game on that computer, and it was that game that got me into college…. Because Jay wrote the letter." A strange sensation made his back sort of tingle. "I never really thought about it, but Jay's been responsible for a lot of things in my life. He wasn't just my first love; he also showed me that I wasn't alone. He was there for me when my mother told me she had cancer, and he was there when I said goodbye to her." And now he'd been there on the day Don learned he had cancer.

"That's so romantic." Bobbi practically batted her eyes at him.

"I know it sounds that way, but like I said, it's been a lot of years. I don't even know that he's single or still interested in anything beyond being friends," Donald told her. "Hell, I don't even know him anymore. The person I knew is sort of stuck in time from ten years ago, and there's been a lot of water under the bridge for both of us since then." He finished the last bite of his salad and then threw the plastic container into the trash, figuring if he didn't take a minute to collect his thoughts he wouldn't have any secrets left.

"But he asked you to dinner, and he understands what you're going through. So it's been a long time—what does that matter? You get the chance to get to know him all over again, and if he just wants to be friends, you can never have too many of those," Bobbi pronounced with authority. "We should get back to work."

They both got up, walked to their area, and scanned their cards to gain access before settling at their desks and getting started.

For most of the afternoon, Donald was about as productive as a hair dryer in a hurricane, between thoughts of having dinner with Jay, wondering about enough things to think he'd been struck stupid, and worrying about the cancer and his surgery next week. He couldn't do anything about the surgery or the cancer, and he realized he couldn't do anything about Jay, either, except show up for dinner.

When the end of the workday finally came around, they locked up all their work and made sure everything was secure before leaving the office. The others said good night and headed home while Donald walked to his car after showing Bobbi that he was gratefully wearing her birthday present. At least he felt warm while outdoors for the first time in weeks. "Thank you, Bobbi," he said to himself as he opened his car door and got inside. The car door closed with a mellow thunk that he loved. Up to now, Donald had always had inexpensive used cars, but a few months ago he'd purchased his first new car, and he loved it. His Taurus wasn't flashy or fancy, but it was comfortable and it was all his... well, his and the bank's. He started the engine, carefully pulling out of the parking lot, and drove to the restaurant.

Donald parked on the street and walked inside, looking around the bright, cheerful dining room before he started removing his layers. "Donny," he heard from behind him, and he turned as Jay took off his coat, draping it over his arm. "It's so good to see you," Jay said, pulling him into a hug.

"It's good to see you too," Donald said automatically, closing his eyes as Jay's familiar scent filled his nose. It might have been years, but there were things about Jay that Donald would always remember—his scent, his smile, and the way he held him. Even their brief hug triggered memories.

"Table for two," Jay told the hostess, and she led them through the restaurant. "Thank you," Jay told her, and they sat down. "I can't believe it's you," Jay told him excitedly.

"I can't believe you're working with my oncologist. You told me you were going to specialize."

"Well, I sort of did it for your mom. She had an impact on my life, and I wanted to help people like her. I had no idea that someday I'd be helping you. Are you going to be okay?" Jay asked, and Donald nodded.

"I think so. There's nothing I can do but take care of myself." Donald did not want to talk about his tumor. It made for boring dinner conversation. "So tell me everything," Donald said with a smirk, and he saw Jay shake his head.

"God, I missed you."

"I've missed you too," Donald said with a grin as some of the nervousness he'd felt began to slip away. "I've thought about you a lot."

"I've thought about you too," Jay said as the server approached. She took their drink order before leaving, and the table fell silent. Donald wasn't sure what to say. He had so many questions, but he wasn't sure he had a right to ask them. In the past, they had always been open with each other, but too much time had passed for Donald to feel the easy companionship they'd once had.

"I'm sorry, I should...," they both said at the same time, and then they laughed. Donald motioned for Jay to go ahead.

"I should have kept in touch," Jay told him. "I feel really bad about that, because...." The server set their drinks on the table, and Jay took a gulp from his martini glass. "Because...."

"What happened, Jay?" Donald said, seeing the pain in his friend's eyes.

"My father cut me off about a year ago. He found out I was seeing someone, and we haven't spoken since. At the time it was very traumatic. Not that the relationship lasted very long after that." Jay set down his glass. "You know, I always thought I was using him and didn't care, but I did. He was my father, and he should have loved me, no matter what."

Donald's heart did a little skip, because in that expression he saw the Jay he knew, the caring person he'd originally fallen in love with. "How are you handling it now that some time has passed?"

"Better," Jay told him. "It still hurts, but not as badly. My mother calls me every now and then, though she makes sure my father doesn't know. It's funny, but growing up I sort of thought she really didn't care, but she does. I'm sort of wondering now how long she'll stay with my father." Jay took another sip from his glass, but some of the hurt remained on his face. "What about you? What are you doing here?"

"I got transferred here about six months ago, and I'm working on something for the Defense Department, but that's all I can say. I love it, though, and everything had been going really well until—" Donald cut himself off as he found himself returning to the subject of his cancer. "You know what I miss most about being here? Being near the water and not being able to go crabbing and all the things I used to do. I haven't done those things in a while, and I miss it. I went fishing last summer a few times, but it wasn't the same."

"I miss it too. But mostly I miss the person I used to go crabbing with. I love my job, and I think I can really make a difference, but I miss some of the things I used to do," Jay said before adding, "that *we* used to do."

The server approached the table, and Donald realized he hadn't even looked at the menu. He read for a minute and then placed his order. Jay did the same, and then the server left, looking a bit miffed. Donald realized he was staring at Jay, and looked away with a sigh. "Being here with you is strange," Donald blurted, figuring he'd go for broke. "Every time I think about you or see you, I keep expecting the same person I knew when we were younger, and that isn't fair to you or to me. At least my head keeps saying that, while my heart keeps bringing up the old feelings that it won't let die." Donald half expected Jay to laugh at him, but he didn't. Instead, he nodded slowly. "I have a friend I work with, Bobbi, and she told me that first love was very powerful."

"I think she's right," Jay said as he reached across the table, taking Donald's hand.

Instantly, Donald closed his eyes, and he was transported back to when they were kids. Jay's touch felt the same, and the way his thumb rubbed the back of Donald's hand was so familiar. "I wish I knew what kind of hold you have on my heart," Donald said as he slowly pulled his hand back, opening his eyes just in time to see the disappointment on Jay's face. "It's been ten years, and all you have to do is touch my hand and my heart speeds up." Donald reached for the water on the table, feeling very warm all of a sudden.

"Then what does this do?" Jay asked before leaning close to him. Donald felt his warm breath on his skin, and then Jay was kissing him. Instantly, it felt like he'd been hit by a jolt of electricity that lasted until Jay pulled away.

"Jay," Donald said softly. "You make every cell in my body jump, but I don't know if it's because of what we once had or attraction to the man you are now. I don't know how it can be anything other than what we meant to each other, because I don't really know you now." He was babbling and he knew it, but he couldn't seem to turn the words off. He wanted so badly to have everything be the way it was and to know that Jay loved him and that he loved Jay for the person he was, but there were so many questions.

"Yes, you do, just like I know you," Jay told him. "You're kind and giving, with a huge heart. When you love, you love with everything you have. You love riding your bicycle, catching crabs, developing video games, and no one has ever looked at me the way you look at me. You know me almost better than I know myself."

"That's just it, I don't, and that's what confuses me, because I keep expecting to," Donald said, and he heard Jay chuckle.

"Maybe you're right," Jay told him with a glint in his eye, "and maybe you're not. Only time will tell." Donald couldn't help smiling at Jay's hint that they would be seeing each other again.

Their server began delivering their food, and the conversation tapered off for a few minutes while they ate. "So what was medical school like?" Donald asked.

"Grueling." Jay's eyes lit up. "I've never worked so hard at anything in my life, and I loved every minute of it. Every day was a challenge, and I felt exhausted, excited, pumped, and drained all at the same time. I'll admit, I had an edge on some of the other students because I grew up in a house with a doctor, so a lot of the basic information was familiar because Dad talked about it all the time. But that advantage didn't last long amid the fierce competition among the students."

"Sounds like you were in your element," Donald said. "I bet you're going to make an amazing doctor."

"I'd like to think so. I'm working hard, and I hope I'll be able to continue to work with Dr. Rivers. He's an amazing oncologist, and there's so much I can learn from him." Jay took a bite of his croquette and swallowed. "What about you? Do you like what you're doing?"

"I love it. I can't talk about it much. But I get to use the same skills I did with the games. It's really cool." Donald hated that he couldn't talk about his work with Jay, but he knew he had to be careful or he could lose his security clearance. "I have started thinking about developing a new game, though. I haven't decided what I want to do yet."

"You were always good at those," Jay said. "Say, do you still have *Catching Crabs*?" Jay's smile was infectious.

"Yes, somewhere. I looked at it a while ago, and it seemed strange. Like it was from another time, and I guess it was. I still can't believe you sent the game and a letter in my name to Virginia Tech."

"You were brilliant, are brilliant, and someone besides me needed to see it. I didn't do anything you couldn't have done yourself."

"Maybe not, but you were the one who did it, and because of that I was able to get a college education." Donald still choked up a bit when he thought about it. What Jay had done was one of the kindest and most thoughtful things anyone had ever done for him. "I've been thinking of returning to school for a master's degree in a few years. I liked school, and Rockwell will pay for most of the tuition, so I only need to find the time." Donald ate a few bites as the conversation slowed a little. The silences felt comfortable, and Donald found he was studying Jay. He'd definitely grown up and was even more handsome. They talked about everything, and when the server took their plates away and brought coffee, they continued talking for what seemed only like a few minutes, but when Donald checked his watch, he realized they'd been sitting for two hours.

Jay stood up and excused himself. While he was gone, the server brought the check, and Donald handed her his credit card. "Hey, I asked you to dinner," Jay told him when he returned.

"You can get the next one," Donald said, and Jay smiled.

Donald bundled himself up and headed out into the cold evening with Jay behind him. It had begun to snow lightly, and Donald took a second to watch the flakes fall. "I'm parked right over here," Donald said, and Jay looked in the direction he indicated, but didn't move away. He could feel Jay's warmth, and it deepened when Jay moved closer and hugged him tight. Donald relished the closeness, but Jay didn't stop there. Donald felt a soft, gloved hand under his chin, and Jay tilted his head up slightly before kissing him.

"I missed you more than I can say, Donny. There were few days that I didn't think of you and wish I was with you," Jay told him.

"Then why didn't you contact me?" Donald asked, looking into Jay's eyes.

"I didn't want to intrude into your life. It had been so long," Jay said, and Donald moved forward, and kissed Jay hard. He'd kissed other men, but none of them felt like Jay. Five years earlier, he'd turned Jay down and sort of pushed him away because he didn't think he could take the rejection and heartache of Jay leaving again. But he'd still gone, and Donald had still felt the same loneliness. He wouldn't make that mistake again. Jay immediately responded to the kiss, returning it, deepening it. Their tongues dueled, and Donald sucked on Jay's lower lip as they stood on the sidewalk, the snow falling around them.

"I live just a few miles south of here. You can follow me if you like," Donald offered tentatively.

Jay said he had a GPS, so Donald gave him the address and then got in the car. He drove cautiously, and when he pulled up in front of his small bungalow home, Jay was waiting for him in his car. As Donald stepped up the snowy walk, another car came down the street, and stopped right behind Jay's. Donald waited at the top of the steps, watching as Jay got out of his car. "Hello, Mrs. Burke," Donald called as his neighbor carefully picked her way to the sidewalk in her old-fashioned galoshes.

Jay turned and hurried over to her, taking Mrs. Burke's arm and guiding her up the walk to her front door. Donald couldn't hear what they were saying to one another. But he saw his sweet, hunched-over neighbor pat Jay on the arm before going into her house. Jay then crossed the street, and Donald watched as he bounded up the walk. He was the same Jay he remembered.

Donald unlocked the door and went inside. The first thing he did was turn up the heat before taking off his outer layers. He'd barely hung up his coat when Jay slipped his arms around his waist, and he felt Jay's chest against his back. "You smell so good," Jay said from behind him, and Donald leaned back into the embrace, instantly trusting him. Jay pulled Donald's shirttail out of his pants, and Donald shivered, but not from the cold, as Jay stroked the skin of his belly. "It's been a long time since I've been able to touch you like this."

"I know," Donald murmured, his eyes closing as Jay traced little circles on his skin. Jay's touch moved upward, fingers passing over one of his nipples, and Donald groaned softly. It had been a while since he'd been touched, and nothing compared to this. He'd been intimate with other guys, he'd even had a few boyfriends, but there was something in the way Jay touched him with just the right combination of firm softness that had him shaking.

Before he knew it, Jay was leading him through the room to the sofa against the living room wall. Donald hadn't even been looking where he was going, and then he plopped down, with Jay on top of him, insistent lips kissing him hard. Jay's weight pressed him into the cushions, and Donald began grabbing at Jay's shirt, pulling it out of his pants in a near frantic effort to get to his skin. Jay knelt on the cushions, straddling Donald, as his shirt was taken off. Jay tugged Donald's sweater and shirt over his head. Then he was back, their chests pressing together. Donald didn't want to move; Jay felt so good moving against him. For weeks, Donald had never felt warm, but right now he was hot, and he wanted more so badly he could taste it.

When Jay stood up, Donald groaned at the loss—of the warmth, the touch, Jay's lips against his. Donald sat up quickly, wondering what was wrong, and Jay sat back down, tugging him onto his lap. Donald felt a bit foolish being held this way—that is, until Jay pulled him into another kiss. Then all thoughts disappeared, and when Jay smoothed him back down onto the cushions, rubbing his hands lightly up and down Donald's chest, Donald arched his back without even thinking about it, and Jay ghosted his fingers along Donald's belly, just above his belt. "You are still the most beautiful man I have ever seen," Jay told him in his deep, resonant voice. "And I like you this way, laid out for me like a beautiful buffet." Donald laid his head against the armrest, looking up as Jay gazed at him. Jay opened his belt, and Donald's breath hitched. "I like it when you shiver for me."

"You could always make me shake," Donald moaned as the fastener on his pants opened and Jay slipped the zipper down, parting the fabric. Jay teased under the band of his boxers before sliding his fingers inside.

"Lift your hips, Donny," Jay said, and his pants and underwear slid just below his butt. Donald's cock throbbed in the cool air, jumping and bouncing against his belly. "You were always amazing, and you never knew it," Jay said, and Donald felt his heart race at the words. He'd always thought he was average, but Jay had never failed to make him feel special. Maybe that was why he'd always loved him too much, and why he'd held on to that love over the years.

Jay closed his fingers around his length, holding him tightly. "Jay, please," Donald begged in a raspy voice. He knew he sounded a bit desperate, but he'd waited a very long time for Jay to touch him again, and he wanted more, he wanted it all.

"You'll get everything you want and more tonight. But right now, I want your pleasure in my hands." Jay leaned toward Donald. "I want you to know how I have always felt about you. That I love you, Donny, and that I've always loved you." Slowly, Jay moved his hand, and Donald groaned deeply, trying to buck his hips for more, but Jay anticipated every move he made and kept him under his control. "I love this spot right here," Jay told him, his thumb lightly caressing the spot just below the head on the underside of his cock.

"That's not fair," Donald cried even as he tried to thrust up into the touch.

"Sure it is," he said soothingly. "I remember everything about you. I always have." Jay gripped his cock in a fist, holding him still as he shifted slightly, leaning over him before running his tongue around a nipple. "See, I remembered that doing this long enough is almost enough to make you come," Jay whispered before doing it again, and Donald felt a zing slide along his spine.

"And I remember that your nipples aren't sensitive, but that divot above your hip will drive you crazy," Donald countered, and he saw Jay's eyes darken. He reached to Jay's face, running his hand along his cheek before stroking lightly behind his ears. "I also remember this little spot and the way you loved it when I kissed you right here."

Jay moaned and stroked him harder, which was the exact effect Donald had been hoping to have. Donald could feel Jay's cock pressing against his butt through his pants, and Donald ground himself onto it, hearing Jay hiss softly. "So that's how it is," Jay teased. Jay continued stroking him, then worked his other hand slowly beneath him, and pressed a finger to the sensitive skin of his opening. Donald forgot about anything other than Jay's touch and the tingling sensations that reverberated through his body. He wasn't going to last long, but Jay seemed to know that already. He seemed to touch him in just the right way to send the maximum amount of stimulation and pleasure through him.

Donald's eyes clamped shut, his breathing becoming ragged as he tried to hold off his impending climax as long as possible to maximize the feeling. Jay, on the other hand, had different ideas, and he stroked him harder and faster, paying special attention to the head of his cock. Unable to contain it any longer, Donald exploded, feeling the warmth of his release as it coated his stomach.

He didn't move, letting the rush of endorphins carry him away for as long as it would last. Slowly he came back to himself, and when he opened his eyes, he saw Jay, a pleased smile shining at him. "You're amazing," Jay told him, and Donald was about to protest that he wasn't the one who was amazing, but gave up. Words didn't immediately come to mind for what he'd just experienced.

"I love you, Jay," Donald managed to say, and he felt Jay shift beneath him until he was close enough that they could kiss. "I always have."

"I know, because I love you too," Jay said before kissing him hard. They both shifted, and soon Jay was holding him, his hands stroking Donald's back.

"I think we should move to the bedroom," Donald suggested, and Jay agreed with a nod. Donald slowly got to his feet, his pants pooling around his ankles. He toed off his shoes and stepped out of his clothes, using his shirt to wipe himself before walking through the house to his bedroom.

"You have a great butt," Jay said from behind him, and Donald jumped and squeaked when Jay grabbed it.

"You're being naughty," Donald scolded with a chuckle as Jay drew him into his arms, a warm chest pressing to his back. Donald shivered and Jay began rubbing his arms.

"You're cold," Jay commented softly, and Jay hurried them into the bedroom and tugged down the covers. Donald climbed into the bed, watching as Jay stripped off the last of his clothes before joining him. "Is this better?" Jay asked, spooning to his back, rubbing his hands over his skin. Donald murmured his assent, snuggling as close to Jay as possible and trying not to shiver too much. Rolling over, Donald once again snuggled close as Jay worked one leg between his.

Jay had always been bigger than Donald, and he used that size to roll him onto his back. Brown eyes stared down at Donald, and Jay smiled as their hips and cocks slid against one another. They didn't talk, and for that Donald was grateful. Instead, Jay let his body speak for him. "Roll over, sweetheart," Jay murmured, and Donald did as he asked, feeling Jay kiss and lick his way down his back. Jay's tongue blazed a hot trail down his lower back before settling in the small of his back, just above his butt.

Feeling Jay's hands massaging his cheeks, Donald thrust his butt back into the touch. Jay licked one of his cheeks, and then Donald felt teeth lightly scrape his skin. "What are you doing?"

"Butt hickey," Jay answered, and Donald chuckled as Jay gave the other cheek the same treatment. "Matched set of perfect cheeks," Jay commented. Donald wasn't sure what he expected, but it wasn't for Jay to spread his cheeks.

"Jesus, Jay!" Donald called as Jay's tongue zeroed in on his opening.

"Hasn't anyone ever done this?" Jay asked, blowing on Donald's wet skin, sending a shiver through him.

"Not since you," Donald confessed. Jay chuckled, and Don heard something like, "Good, this is mine," and then he felt Jay nibbling and licking his skin. Donald ground himself into the sheets, moaning and whimpering loudly. Jay smoothed his hands down his thighs, and Donald spread his legs further. He felt completely wanton, and Jay made every second worth it.

"You don't act this way all the time?" Jay asked, hot breath kissing his wet skin.

"Only with you," Donald answered, and he moaned as Jay dipped one finger inside him and then pulled out. "Tease," he accused, and Jay chuckled.

"That's right. I'll tease, taste, and even tickle you into complete oblivion before I'm done. Remember, I'm a doctor and I know exactly how to drive you crazy."

"Prove it," Donald challenged him, and very soon he wished he hadn't. Jay used his magic tongue and a finger to drive Donald out of his mind. It got to the point that every touch, no matter how innocent, made his skin tingle. "Jay," Donald pleaded, wriggling his butt in what he hoped was an enticing way because he wasn't sure how much more of this he could take. As it turned out, quite a lot, because Jay drove him to the brink and then pulled him back over and over. By the time Jay let him roll over, Donald could barely remember his name, and he was wound so tight, he begged Jay to fuck him.

"Oh, I will, sweetheart, don't you worry," Jay told him. "Do you have anything?"

Donald pulled open a drawer and then heard Jay fish around. He must have found a condom and the lube, because Donald felt him straighten up, and after a bit of fumbling, Jay lifted Donald's legs to his shoulders and pressed into him. Once Jay started, there was no stopping him. He pressed deep and hard, taking Donald's breath away as he was filled and stretched. Then Jay began to move.

This was no gentle lovemaking, but a full-on, take him to heaven fucking. Donald gripped the sheets for dear life as Jay drilled into him. "I've dreamed about being inside you for ten years," Jay hissed through clenched teeth as he snapped his hips, pegging Donald's gland so hard he cried out in ecstatic surprise. After experiencing God's gift in foreplay, Donald didn't think he could possibly be driven higher, but Jay managed to do it over and over again. This time he didn't back off one bit. "Don't touch yourself," Jay commanded when Donald reached for his cock. "I want you to come just from me. You're the most beautiful man on earth, and you're all mine."

That was just what Donald had longed to hear for a decade. Tears formed in his eyes as his body hummed with energy, but he couldn't quite get enough, his release seeming just out of reach. "I can't," Donald said breathlessly, fighting the urge to reach for himself. His brain felt like it was on fire, and he needed some relief.

"Yes, you can. Show me how I've made you feel and how much you needed me." Jay leaned over him, snapping his hips as his fingers plucked at Don's nipples just the way he liked it.

"I can't," Donald cried even as his mind and body tripped over the edge, and he tumbled into a mind-numbing orgasm that left him seeing stars. He could barely catch his breath, and for a few seconds Donald wondered what was happening, and then the happy tingly feeling kicked in, and Donald was floating. He stayed that way for the longest time, with only Jay intruding on his euphoric delusions. He felt and heard his lover's climax, which only heightened his own.

Eventually Donald felt Jay's weight on top of him, his arms wrapping around him, and then Jay nestled against him. They lay together without moving for a long time. Donald was warm in Jay's arms, and every breath he took resulted in a dose of Jay's magnificent musk filling his nose. "Can you stay?" Donald asked, and he felt rather than heard Jay's affirmative answer. Donald was about to pull up the blankets, but before he could move, he felt Jay get out of the bed. Hearing his footsteps grow fainter, Donald cracked his eyes open, watching Jay's bare butt as he made his way to the bathroom. Water ran, and then footsteps approached.

A warm cloth stroked over his skin, and Donald stretched, enjoying that someone was pampering him just a little. No one had done that in a very long time. A dry towel moved over his skin, and then Jay was gone once again. Jay was beautiful as he moved in the dim light from a small lamp. Donald watched as each muscle moved and flowed, like those of a powerful, huge cat. That was it—Jay was his lion. Donald smiled at the thought as he waited for Jay to return.

The light clicked out, and then Jay was in bed with him, holding him, keeping him warm as the wind whistled outside the house. "Do you realize this is the first time we've ever slept together?" Donald asked. "We were never able to sleep together like this when we were together as teenagers."

"I know. There are definite advantages to getting older," Jay said, and Donald snuggled closer.

Donald got quiet and his thoughts began to wander. "Sometimes I'm afraid I'm going to die," Donald said softly into the darkness. "I have cancer and I know that's what killed my mother. I keep trying to tell myself that it's not going to happen to me, but it still scares me."

"I know," Jay told him. "But I'm not going to let that happen. The tumor's going to be removed, and you're going to be healthy and strong." Jay's voice sounded sure and confident.

Donald rolled over to face Jay. "I'm going to have to have chemo. That means all my hair is going to fall out. Do you think I'm going to look good bald?"

"You'll be beautiful no matter what," Jay said softly. "Are you going to wait for it to fall out?"

"No." Donald tilted his face so he was facing Jay. "I was hoping you'd help me shave my head. I've decided that I'm going to wear it like a badge of honor. From everything I've read, it's going to be an ordeal, and like warriors, I'm going to wear my battle scars with pride."

"Good," Jay said, and Donald felt Jay stroking his hair. "I know this will be gone for a while, but it'll grow back, and you'll get better. You won't have to go through this alone. I can promise you that." Jay held him close, and the room got quiet.

Donald felt better just knowing that Jay would be there for him. He didn't have illusions that he and Jay were together, no matter what Jay said, but he felt better knowing that Jay wanted to pursue a relationship. He'd felt alone for a long time, but now he wasn't alone. At one of the scariest and most troubling times of his life, he wasn't alone. Jay was here with him, just like he'd been for many of the great moments in his life. Whatever twist of fate had put him in Jay's path and kept doing it amazed him, because he had to be the luckiest person alive.

"Go to sleep, Donny," Jay told him, and Donald closed his eyes. But he didn't want to go to sleep. Having Jay with him, lying next to him, was too good to just let happen while he slept. So Donald closed his eyes and listened to Jay breathe, smiling to himself. Eventually, Donald drifted off to sleep, dreaming of Jay, nestled in his warmth.

A rush of cool air threatened to wake him, but then the warmth returned, and Donald burrowed beneath the covers. Moving over, he reached out for Jay, but felt only the bedding. He patted the mattress a few times and then opened his eyes, realizing that Jay was no longer in bed with him. Sitting up, he listened, but the house was quiet. Getting out of bed, he tugged on his robe and wandered through the house, peering out the front window. The dark form that should have been Jay's car was gone, and Donald felt his heart sink. Jay was gone again. Shuffling back to the bed, Donald turned on the light and saw a piece of paper on the pillow Jay had used.

I had to go, but I'll see you soon. Didn't want to wake you. Love, Jay.

Donald went back to bed with a smile on his face.

DAY 6

THREE WEEKS LATER
MILWAUKEE, WI

"How are you feeling?" Bobbi asked as she approached his desk. She'd been his rock for the past three weeks.

Donald looked up from his workstation. "I'm better. The incision is healed, and they put in the port when they took out the tumor. The first chemo treatment knocked me for a loop, but Dr. Rivers said it's mainly a precaution, so he's not using something really strong. I have an appointment this afternoon, and at least three more treatments. Then he'll evaluate where we go from there, but the doctor is hopeful, and so am I." Donald had been working as much as he could, but only managed a few days a week.

"You don't look hopeful," Bobbi countered. "You look like you lost your best friend." She patted him lightly on the shoulder. "Maybe you should rest before you go in for your checkup."

Donald patted her hand. Bobbi was turning into a real mother hen as far as he was concerned, though to Donald's surprise, he liked it, especially since Jay…. "I'm fine. I'll probably take tomorrow off so I can rest, but I should be back to work after that." Bobbi looked at him like she didn't believe it, and Donald knew he was probably trying to do too much too soon. He got tired at the most surprising times.

"Take whatever time you need. The project isn't due for months, and we're ahead of schedule, largely thanks to you. We all want you well." Bobbi went back to her desk, and Donald tried to go back to the configurable setting for the flight controls that he'd been working on for weeks. He was so close he could taste it. His phone rang and Donald pulled it out of his pocket, answering it without looking at who was calling.

"This is Donald," he said as happily as he could.

"This is Susan in Dr. Rivers's office. You have an appointment this afternoon, but he was wondering if you would be available to come in this morning." Susan always sounded like she was smiling.

"Sure. When do you want me to come in?" Donald asked as he looked at Bobbi, who nodded her understanding.

"As soon as you can get here," Susan said apologetically.

"It's no problem, I'll be right over," Donald said, and he began closing down his files and getting ready to leave. All the members of the team said goodbye and wished him luck. He'd told Randy and the colonel about his cancer shortly before having the surgery, and everyone had been supportive. Randy's wife had even sent in homemade soup for him. Donald put on his coat and got ready to brave the cold. Before he left, Bobbi gave him a hug and a smile of solidarity. "Thanks, Bobbi."

"Call and let me know what happens," Bobbi told him, and Donald agreed before leaving the office and going to his car. He arrived at the doctor's office a few minutes later, and after checking in with the receptionist, he sat down to wait. He didn't wait long before he was called back and ushered into an examination room.

"How are you, Mary?" Donald asked as the nurse began taking his blood pressure.

"I'm good. How are you? Any pain?" she asked as she recorded the result and then got ready to take his pulse.

"A little, but it gets better every day," Donald said. "Do you need blood this time?"

"Yes. Dr. Rivers wants to check things before we do another round of chemo," Mary explained, and then drew blood as painlessly as she usually did, making more notes in her computer. "He'll be right in," Mary said, and Donald nodded, remembering the last time he was in this examination room. The door had opened and he'd seen Jay again for the first time in five years. But after spending an amazing night together and waking up to Jay's note, he'd heard nothing at all. Don had kept expecting Jay to call him. In his surprise and haste, he hadn't gotten Jay's phone number. He'd tried looking him up on the Internet, but he hadn't had any luck. Truthfully, he figured Jay had decided he wasn't interested after he left, and Donald had tried coming to terms with that, particularly after the things they'd said to one another. He'd been dumped before, but being treated this way by Jay had hurt, so he'd done his best to try to put it behind him. He knew he wasn't doing a very good job of it, though.

When the examination door opened, Dr. Rivers walked in and began the exam. "I'm sorry about the change in schedule," the doctor said as he sat down.

"It's no problem," Donald said. "So how am I doing?"

"Very well. All indications are that we got the entire tumor, so all we need to do is make sure there's no residual cancer in your body." He had Donald lie back on the table, and he inspected the incision, which was nearly completely healed, and the port looked good. He also did a general examination. "We'll make a final decision based upon your blood work, but I'd like to schedule you for the next treatment on Monday. You're responding well. Have there been any side effects?"

"Other than nausea for a few days and being tired, no," Donald said. He'd heard the stories, and he considered himself pretty lucky that he was feeling as good as he was.

"Excellent," Dr. Rivers said as he felt around Donald's stomach and neck. He listened to his lungs and heart before pressing against his sides. "I'm very pleased. Everything is going as we expected." Donald sat back up and put his shirt back on while the doctor made notes in his computer. "I'd like to see you again after the next treatment," the doctor told him. "And I want you to be sure to get plenty of rest."

"I will," Donald promised. The doctor left the room, and Donald gathered his things and walked toward the front desk, where he saw Susan. "I need to make an appointment for after my next treatment, which he scheduled for Monday."

"Sure," she said with a smile and began working at her terminal. "How about next Friday at two?" Susan asked.

"Perfect," Donald told her, and he turned to look back down the hall and through the office. He kept looking for Jay, expecting to see him at any moment. Not that he knew what he would say to him, other than probably yell and have to restrain himself from punching Jay in his perfect teeth.

"Is there something I can help you with?" Susan asked, and Donald saw her following his gaze.

"No, sorry," he said and turned back to her. "I was just wondering where the intern was." Donald hoped he was keeping it cool and didn't sound too desperate, but he was really curious where Jay was. Donald expected her to tell him that Jay had gone back to school or was working in one of the hospitals. He figured that just like the other times they'd gotten together, something had once again pulled Jay away from him.

"Oh, honey," Susan said, her eyes full of concern. "It's so sad." She stopped what she was doing and leaned close, looking round the office. "He was paged in to the hospital a few weeks ago and got into an accident. It was the middle of the night, and the roads were slippery." She looked like she'd suddenly gone into mourning, and Donald's heart fell to the floor. That night, the accident, it had to have been after Jay had left him the note. "The accident was bad and...." She sniffled and Donald closed his eyes.

"Jay's dead?" he asked softly, trying to hold out hope even as the things he'd been carrying in his arms fell to the floor. Jay was gone, and Donald had thought he'd left him when instead he'd been hurt and had probably died alone. Donald felt tears sting the back of his eyes, and his throat closed up. Jay was gone and he hadn't had a chance to say goodbye.

Susan shook her head. "No. But he's been in the hospital in a coma for weeks, and they don't know if he'll recover." Susan reached for a tissue and blew her nose. "He was the kindest man," Susan said as she wiped her eyes. "He went out of his way to be nice and help people. My daughter was born with a cleft palate, and he helped me get in touch with a plastic surgeon who could help her. The insurance company didn't want to pay because they said it wasn't that bad and they considered it cosmetic. Dr. Jason made a few phone calls and yelled at a few people, and now she'll have the surgery in a few weeks, and the insurance company is going to pay for it." Susan blew her nose again.

That certainly sounded like the Jay he knew. The one who had sent the letter that had helped get him into college. "Which hospital is he at?" Donald asked as he tried to pick up the things he'd dropped, his heart racing and his head spinning. He had to get over there right away.

"St. Luke's," she answered, dabbing her eyes. Donald grabbed his things and started walking toward the door. "I have your appointment card," Susan called to him, and Donald rushed back and took the card before hurrying out the door to his car. The fatigue that he'd been feeling was gone as his heart raced and adrenaline pounded through his body. He didn't even stop long enough to pull on his gloves and hat, not feeling the cold at all.

Donald drove as fast as he dared, silently telling Jay that he was on his way, between bouts of beating himself up for not looking harder to find him. Jay had been lying in a hospital bed for weeks, and during that entire time Donald had been angry with him because he'd thought Jay had rejected him. He didn't know for sure how Jay really felt, but Donald knew what he himself felt, and he intended to move heaven and earth to see and talk to Jay. Parking in the hospital lot, Donald slammed the car door before hurrying toward the hospital entrance. He gave his name at the visitor's desk and asked to see Jason Greene. He was told he was in intensive care, and Donald took the card he was given and followed the directions to the fourth floor.

The elevator door opened, and Donald stepped out into a waiting room, where he saw Jay's mother sitting in a chair, looking nervous. She saw him and looked twice, as if he was familiar but she couldn't quite place him. Donald took a deep breath, unsure about the kind of reception he was going to get, and walked into the seating area.

"Mrs. Greene." She looked at him and lifted herself out of the chair. "You probably don't remember me. I'm Donald Pottier. Jay and I were friends on Chincoteague." He figured he would play it as low-key as possible. "How is Jay? I just heard about what happened to him."

She looked tired and frazzled. "I thought you looked familiar. It's been a long time," she said softly but coolly.

"Ten years. I've seen Jay a few times. The last one was the day of his accident," Donald said in the hushed room.

She sighed softly and almost collapsed back into the chair. She obviously hadn't been sleeping much lately. "He's awake, but he doesn't remember anything. It's like most of his life is gone. He remembers his name and small bits and pieces of things, but nothing else." She pulled a tissue out of her purse. "He doesn't know me or his father." She dabbed her eyes, and Donald could see that the tears were very close to the surface. "My own son doesn't remember me. He knows he has a mother, but he hasn't made the connection that I'm her."

The door to the waiting room opened, and Donald saw Dr. Greene stride in as though he owned the place. He looked at his wife and then at Donald. "There isn't any change," he said to her before settling his attention on Donald. "Elliot Greene," he said, extending his hand.

"I'm Donald Pottier. I knew your son from the summers he spent on Chincoteague." Donald reached for his hand, but it was immediately pulled back, and Dr. Greene's eyes narrowed.

"I know exactly who you are and what you did to my son," Dr. Green growled just above a whisper.

"I didn't do anything to Jay except love him," Donald said as evenly as he could, looking longingly toward the door to the ward. He desperately wanted to see Jay but realized he wasn't going to be given that chance unless Jay parents agreed.

"You turned my son gay," he accused, and Donald nearly laughed. The idea that anyone could turn someone gay was so ridiculous, especially coming from a highly trained and intelligent doctor.

"You know that's not possible. Either Jay is gay or he isn't," Donald replied, staring into Dr. Greene's eyes. He refused to back down like a scared child. "Jay and I loved each other. I know you think we were playing around or something, but we weren't. We loved each other then, and we still do, and you can't change that."

"You never loved my son. You hurt him and turned him against me," Dr. Greene said more quietly.

"How could I have turned Jay against you when you took him away from me and I didn't see or hear from him for five years?" Donald could feel years of anger and resentment for what Jay's father had done to him, and to Jay, bubble to the surface. "If anyone turned him against you, it was you. Jay is gay, and you forced him to hide a big part of who he was from you."

"I did not," Dr. Green countered lamely, sounding rather juvenile.

"I'm afraid you did," Jay's mother said from behind her husband. "Jay was never the same after you dragged him home that summer, and you know it, Elliot," she said, her eyes hard as stone. "Some of the happiness and light drained out of him and never returned. You tried to make him into what you wanted him to be, and it failed miserably."

"I did what was right," Dr. Greene pronounced highhandedly.

"Right for you, just like always. Everything has always been about what you wanted and what you thought best. Well, your arrogance cost us our son. He hasn't spoken to you in over a year, and I can only talk to him or see him when you aren't around." Donald saw the firelight behind her eyes. "That's right, I've talked to him and seen him, because Jason is my son, and I love him, regardless of what you think." She stepped closer to her husband, and Donald stepped back. He hadn't meant to start a fight between them, and as he watched he realized that this was probably a dispute that had been building for a very long time. "You don't even know him," she continued.

"I certainly do. Because of me he dated that girl through most of college," Jay's father countered superiorly.

"She was a lesbian, Elliott," Jay's mother snapped with a roll of her eyes. "He was using her to fool you into paying his tuition. God, are you completely obtuse?" Her voice was rising, and Donald was glad there was no one else in the waiting room because this was turning into a battle royal.

"You knew?" Elliot accused, so angry he appeared to shake.

"At the time, no." Some of the venom left her voice. "But I figured it out eventually, and he told me when I asked him. That's not what's important. You need to accept who your son is and learn to love him for who he is." She stood toe to toe with her larger husband like an Amazon warrior getting ready for battle. "I made more than my share of mistakes when he was growing up, and so did you." They both quieted and some of the tension dissipated.

Donald cleared his throat softly, and they both turned toward him. "I'd like to see him."

"Absolutely not," Dr. Greene said in almost a yell. The sound of a palm striking flesh echoed off the walls like a gunshot, and he snapped his head around to his wife, rubbing his cheek.

"That's enough, Elliot! I've had it with you controlling Jason's life and mine, so back off or you'll get more than that." She stepped closer, and for a second Donald thought she was going to rip off her husband's balls. Dr. Greene obviously wasn't sure what she was going to do, either, and backed away. "Of course he can see Jason. You forget, he's my son too, and I'm tired of you trying to run our lives." Her voice became loud, and a nurse opened the door. They both quieted, staring daggers at one another until Jay's mother turned away and walked to where Donald stood. He didn't like seeing people fight, but he felt inordinately pleased that Jay's mother seemed to have Jay's interests at heart, unlike his father.

"Come with me. They're going to move him to a regular room later today, now that he's awake," she told him as they reached the door. Donald looked back and saw Jay's father staring at them, looking furious, but thankfully he said nothing more. "I'm calling my lawyer, Elliot. This is the last straw." She pulled open the door, and Donald followed behind her, wondering what exactly had just happened.

"I'm sorry, Mrs. Greene," he said.

"Don't be, and please call me Sheila. That's been coming on for a long time." She led him down the hall toward the entrance to the ward. "Jason remembers bits and pieces, but things seem to be fragmented. They're hoping his memory will come back soon, but no one seems to have the answers right now. Just don't be disappointed if he doesn't remember you."

Donald nodded, feeling tired once again. The rush and adrenaline that had been fueling him had worn off. "I'll try."

She nodded and led him into the ward and down the hallway to a small room. Donald peered inside and saw Jay lying in bed with a machine next to him. "They took out most of the tubes and things a few days ago," Sheila explained. Donald watched Jay sleep. He was bruised and had a still faintly visible black eye. Parts of his face were yellow from what appeared to be fading bruises. "He has a broken leg, which is healing well, as are the other injuries," Sheila told him softly, and Donald stepped into the room.

Jay's eyes slid open, and Donald waited to see what sort of reaction he'd get. Jay stared at Donald for a few seconds but didn't say anything.

"I know you from somewhere," Jay finally said hoarsely, and he tried to shift slightly in the bed.

"I'm Donny," he said, feeling unbelievably heartbroken. Donald had felt that somehow Jay wouldn't forget him and would remember the way they felt about each other.

Jay smiled at him, and some of Donald's disappointment slipped away. Jay remembered something about him. "You look older than I remember," Jay said, and Donny sat in the chair next to the bed. He glanced at Sheila, who stood in the doorway, and saw Jay look at her but register almost no recognition at all. It was like he was looking at a near stranger. "In my mind," Jay said as he turned back to Donald, "you're about sixteen years old."

"Do you remember what we did?"

The yellow tint to Jay's skin darkened as he blushed. "Yes. You were my lover," Jay said matter-of-factly, and Donald heard Sheila gasp softly.

"Yes, I was. You and I were each other's first love. Do you remember the video games we used to play?" Donald figured a trip down memory lane might help.

"Nintendo," Jay said with a smile. "It was my game, and you used to beat me at it." Jay looked at Donald quizzically. "You wrote your own video game," Jay told him, and Donald nodded. "But I can't remember the name."

Donald didn't pressure him. "Do you remember the other things we used to do?" He took Jay's hand and held it in his.

"We rode bikes," Jay said, getting a quizzical look on his face, "and we used to carry nets with us. I remember riding with one, but not what we did with them." Donald tried not to supply the answer and let Jay concentrate. "Did we go fishing?"

"Sometimes," Donald said, "but mostly we used to catch something else." He could see the concentration on Jay's face, like the answer he wanted was just out of reach. "It's okay. I know you'll remember, because my mother made your favorite food out of what we caught."

"Crab cakes," Jay said, and Donald smiled and laughed.

"That's right," Donald said. "You do remember."

"So we… we caught crabs. That's it! We used to get chicken necks at the store and tie them onto strings so we could use them as bait. We kissed for the first time after spending the day crabbing, and I thought my head would never stop spinning. That was after I rescued you from those bullies. Krepke! Harmon Krepke." Jay smiled, and Donald peeked toward Sheila, who had moved into the room and was sitting in a chair near the foot of his bed. She looked like she was about to cry.

"Yes, that's right. Do you remember anything else?" Donald asked.

Jay rolled his head on the pillow. "I can remember the first time we were together, but I can't talk about that with her here." Jay indicated his mother, but with no hint of real recognition.

"Would it be okay if I came to see you again?" Donald asked as one of the nurses came into the room along with Jay's scowling father.

"Of course, Donny. You can visit me anytime." He looked at his dad, but Jay's face held the same blank look he had for his mother.

"Good. I'll be back this afternoon, and we can talk some more. I promise," Donald said, and he saw Jay smile. Then Donald left the room with both of Jay's parents right behind him.

"You won't be coming back," Jay's father said, and Donald turned to him.

"I'll be back because Jay said I can. The nurse heard him." Donald walked into the waiting room followed by Jay's parents.

"Elliot, Jay remembered things," Sheila said.

"I don't care," Elliot said, whirling around to her in a fury.

"I do," Donald said, stepping closer to him. "The nurse heard Jay say that he wanted me to come back, and since he's an adult, you have no say anymore. So I will be back, because Jay wants me to visit, and I'm going to help him get his memory back." Donald swallowed and began to sway a little.

"Are you okay?" Sheila asked as Donald moved to a chair to sit down.

"Yes. The chemo sometimes makes me weak at the weirdest times. I'll be fine." Donald breathed deeply and waited for the slight dizziness to pass. When he felt better, Donald rose and walked toward the elevator, ignoring Jay's father. He had something he needed to do, and nothing was going to stop him, especially not Jay's stupid father. Leaving the hospital, Donald drove home and called Bobbi, letting her know what had happened. He told her he was going to take the rest of the day off, which thankfully didn't surprise her at all.

"I promise you I'll tell you the whole story," Donald told her.

"You'd better," Bobbi told him. "I expect a full report." When Donald disconnected, he went to his bedroom to lie down for a while. The chemo sometimes made him tired at the weirdest times, and he'd already learned not to fight it. If he was tired, he rested, and often felt much better afterward. Pulling back the comforter, Donald took off his shoes and lay on the bed, pulling the warm comforter up over him and quickly falling asleep.

He had dreams of Jay lost and trying to find his way. In the dream, Jay kept calling out for help, but Donald couldn't seem to find a way to help Jay get back to him. He kept getting close, but Jay was caught in some sort of fog, and though Donald could hear his voice getting louder, he could never quite reach him. Donald startled awake and looked around. He was in his bedroom and he was fine, but he had the nearly overwhelming urge to try to help Jay. He got up, put on his shoes, and made his way to the kitchen. After getting a glass of juice, Donald sipped from it before making a very light lunch. He didn't think he could eat very much, but he knew he had to have something. Leaving the sandwich dishes in the sink, Donald went to his room and picked up the wooden box Jay had given him all those years ago. He also grabbed his laptop and spent a few minutes rummaging through a file of CDs to find the one he wanted. Carrying his treasures to the dining room, he set them all on the table before going through the process of getting dressed to go back out in the cold.

The clouds had begun to part, and Donald found the bright sun combined with the cold extremely disconcerting. He kept expecting it to warm up when it got sunny. In the car, he actually had to put on sunglasses because of the glare off the snow. When he arrived at the hospital, he carried his bundle in, and when he checked in at the desk, he found that Jay had been moved to a regular room, so he made his way to that floor. He was relieved when he didn't see Jay's father, but Sheila was in Jay's room, sitting in one of the chairs. "Hi, Donny," Jay said with a grin.

"Hi, Jay. I brought you some things to show you," Donald said. Sheila looked up from the chair as Donald set the laptop on the tray and started it, and once it booted, he inserted the CD.

"I remember this," Jay said with a touch of glee. "It's the game you wrote." Jay played for a while using the keyboard, but he'd definitely lost his edge, and the crabs got too smart and attacked him.

"Do you remember what you did with the game? Who you sent it to?" Donald prompted.

"Are you mad?" Jay asked like he was still sixteen years old.

"No. Who did you send it to?" Donald asked again. He knew Jay seemed to be remembering things, and he wanted him to remember the happy things before the sad things came back.

"Admissions at Virginia Tech," Jay admitted reluctantly. "Did it work?"

"You tell me. You know the answer," Donald replied, and Jay settled his head onto the pillow for a while then he shook his head. "It's okay. You'll remember when the time is right." Donald opened the box he'd brought and pulled out an old miniature golf scorecard and handed it to Jay.

"Pirate Cove Miniature Golf," Jay read off the front. "This is where Krepke worked. You and I played a game here. This game."

"Yes, we did. Do you remember our bet?"

"Loser buys lunch," Jay said with a smile. "I do remember. You won."

"Only because you cheated and took points off my score because you knew I didn't have the money to actually buy lunch. I think that was the moment I completely fell in love with you." Donald took Jay's hand, and he felt Jay's thumb stroke along the back, the way he'd always done. "I remember everything we ever did together." Donald took the scorecard. "Do you remember what's on your back?"

Jay concentrated and Don gently helped him sit up, tracing the familiar design with his finger. "A tattoo," Jay answered.

"Do you remember what's hidden in it?" Don asked as he helped settle Jay back in the bed.

"Your initials. I got it so you'd be with me always," Jay said with almost childish glee, and Sheila stood up. Donald watched her as she walked to Jay's box of tissues, then pulled one out and used it to wipe her eyes.

"I never knew," she said softly. "You boys had a life I never knew about." Donald smiled and nodded slowly before returning to the items in the box.

"Why did you keep all this?" Jay asked as Donald removed two folded pieces of paper.

"You gave me the box, and I put all the things that reminded me of you in it because you would only be with me during the summer." Donald unfolded the pieces of paper. "This may be painful, Jay, but you need to remember." Donald handed Jay the print out of that last e-mail he'd received from Jay ten years earlier.

Jay took the piece of paper and read it. "Did I send this?"

"Yes," Donald said, and he waited and watched as tears formed in Jay's eyes. "You remember, don't you?"

Jay nodded slowly. "Someone told my dad they'd seen us kissing and he…." Jay stopped talking and clamped his eyes shut. Sheila hurried to the bed, but Jay shook his head. "I'm okay, Mom." Sheila stood stock-still.

"You remember me?" Donald thought she was going to cry.

"Yes. I remember Dad hit me and threw my computer out the window so I couldn't talk to Donny, and you did nothing to stop him!" Jay's face turned red, and Donald reached for Jay's hand.

"That was a long time ago, and I'm here with you now. It's okay," Donald soothed. "You need to rest and relax." Jay stared venomously at his mother before looking back at Donald. "Trust me, Jay. You aren't remembering everything, just pieces. We're filling them in together, but you need to trust me. Your mother loves you very much, and that happened a long time ago."

Jay nodded and settled back against the pillow. "Is there more?"

"Do you want to know more?" Donald realized he was taking Jay through the history of their relationship.

"I want to remember everything," Jay said, and Donald handed him a folded bulletin. Jay opened it and looked at Donald. "Your mother died, and I went to the funeral. She had cancer and…." Jay closed his eyes. "I remember, I remember. She told you after we were together for the first time, and I rushed over to be with you after you called." Jay continued staring at the bulletin, turning it over in his hands. "I went to the funeral the year we were both graduating from college," Jay said, and he smiled. "You did get in, and you made your mother proud. She had cancer." Jay looked around the room like he was searching for something. "You have cancer." Jay turned to his mother. "I saw Donny again a few weeks ago at work when he came in for a pretreatment consultation."

"Do you remember being a doctor?" Donald asked, and Jay thought for a few seconds.

"I remember some things, but they're jumbled," Jay said, and Donald nodded.

"That's probably a good sign. You've gotten back a lot of information, though you'll need time to put things back together," Donald said.

Jay smirked wickedly. "When did you go to medical school?" Jay tugged him forward, and Donald placed a light kiss on Jay's lips.

"Do you remember the night before your accident?" Donald whispered as he peered into Jay's eyes, and he saw him nod. "Did you mean what you said?"

"Yes," Jay answered. "Why?"

"You've been here for almost three weeks," Donald told Jay, and he seemed surprised and a bit perplexed.

"So you've had your surgery," Jay said, and Donald nodded, opening his shirt so Jay could see the incision and the port that had been placed in his chest.

"I had my first chemo treatment last week, and I have another one next week. I haven't started losing my hair yet, but that will probably be pretty soon. And I want to remind you about your promise to love me when I'm bald," Donald told him.

"I'll love you no matter what," Jay whispered, and Donald saw Sheila look uncomfortable, but Jay seemed content, and Donald watched as he closed his eyes.

A nurse came into the room, and Donald stepped out, with Sheila following behind him.

"You really love him, as in, getting married, don't you?" Sheila asked.

"Yes, although it's a little soon for that. I've known Jay since I was sixteen, but we haven't spent much time together lately." Donald leaned against the wall as they waited for the nurse to finish. "I know how I've always felt about him. Jay was my first love. He comforted me when my mother told me she had cancer, and he was there when I said goodbye to her." Donald peered into the room, but the nurse was still with Jay, so he returned his attention to Sheila. "Your son is an amazing man, in case you didn't realize it. At seventeen, he sent a letter to Virginia Tech with the video game I created, and that got me a scholarship that allowed me to go to college. He also helped one of the women he works with get the surgery her daughter needed. Jay has the biggest heart of anyone I've ever met, even after his father tried to squeeze it out of him." Donald saw the pained look on Sheila's face, but she needed to hear the truth.

"I had no idea," she whispered, looking at the floor, staring quietly at her shoes.

"I don't want to be mean, but have you taken the time to get to know him? It's obvious his father hasn't." Donald figured he was probably pressing his luck, but he'd do anything for Jay, and if that meant giving his mother a bit of a wakeup call, so be it. Jay had done as much and more for him over the years.

"Sheila," Jay's father said as he strode toward where they were standing. "What is he doing here?"

"We've had this discussion," Sheila said. "Besides, Jay has his memory back, and he can decide who he wants to visit him."

"He can remember?" Elliot asked, and Sheila nodded. Elliot walked toward the door as the nurse came out. They passed each other, and Elliot walked into the hospital room. At first there was silence.

"Get out!" Jay was nearly yelling. "I never want to see you for as long as I live. Go back to Chicago and screw your receptionist, but stay the hell away from me." The nurse and an orderly rushed into the room, and a few seconds later Elliot walked out of the room, glaring at both of them.

"Go home, Elliot," Sheila said firmly, staring him down. He eventually turned and walked toward the elevators, and Donald entered Jay's room. Jay looked relieved and furious.

"He's had enough excitement for one day," the nurse said, and Donald couldn't have agreed more. "I suggest you all let Jason get some rest."

"I'll be back to see you this evening," Donald promised before leaning over the bed to give Jay a kiss. The last one had been gentle, but this one was something very different indeed. "You do realize we have an audience." Jay smiled against his lips, and Donald pulled away.

"Tired?" Jay asked, and Donald nodded.

"I get fatigued at the most inconvenient times." Donald said goodbye and paused at the door to take another look at Jay before leaving. He knew he was being ridiculous, but he didn't want to take the chance that this could be the last time he saw him. They'd had too many last glances and final chances. If something happened this time, Donald knew that would be it. The fates couldn't have that many chances left for them. After smiling at Jay, Donald walked down the hall to the elevator and pressed the call button.

The drive home didn't take long, and he called Bobbi to let her know he was okay and that he hoped to be in to work the following afternoon. After hanging up with her, Donald made a snack and went into the living room. He sat on the sofa, and soon he lay down and fell asleep watching reruns of *Friends*. He woke hungry and decided to get some dinner on his way back to the hospital.

Jay was asleep when he arrived, and Sheila appeared to have left. The hospital room was quiet and dark, so Donald sat in the chair next to the bed, reclining it back, and soon the warmth of the room had him nodding off.

"Donny," he heard Jay say, and he opened his eyes to see Jay smiling brightly at him. "How long have you been here?" Jay asked with a yawn.

"About an hour, I guess," Donald answered, checking his watch. "Have you had anything to eat? I stopped and got something on the way."

"They haven't brought my supper yet, but it's hospital food, so I expect starvation is preferable." Jay chuckled. As if on cue, an orderly brought in Jay's dinner and set it on the tray. Donald got up and moved the tray closer so Jay could eat his dinner. He had to admit it didn't look or smell half-bad. Jay took a bite of what looked like roast beef. "Can I ask you something?"

"Of course."

"I remember what happened now," Jay said. "I'd received a call from Dr. Rivers to meet him at the hospital. I left you the note because I didn't want to wake you." Jay reached over, and Donald took his hand. "You looked so amazingly happy as you slept that I didn't have the heart to wake you. When I got halfway to the hospital, I went through an intersection, and the only other person on the road didn't stop. After that, I woke up here. Did you think I'd forgotten you?"

Donald shook his head. "I thought you'd changed your mind. I tried to find you, but I figured if you weren't interested in me, you didn't need me tracking you down." Donald felt really bad about that now, because if he'd have looked harder, he might have found Jay earlier and he could have been there for him.

"Then how did you find me?" Jay asked.

"I asked Susan in Dr. River's office when I went in for my appointment and didn't see you. She told me what happened, and I hurried right over and ran into the brick wall that is your father." Donald sighed as he thought about the hate and fury in Jay's father's eyes. "He tried to stop your mother from letting me see you, and she slapped him."

"Mom slapped Dad?" Jay asked, and Donald saw his eyes widen as he swallowed a bite of mashed potatoes and made a face. "These taste like glue," Jay groused as he went back to eating the roast beef. "If we got the recipe, we could give it to Elmer's." Donald laughed at Jay's joke.

"Eat your dinner, and tomorrow I'll bring you in something special." Donald moved closer to the bed. "I know they won't be quite the same, but I can make you crab cakes if you're good." Donald remembered how much Jay loved them, and his smile confirmed it, as did the way Jay began shoveling in the food.

"Do you think I'm being foolish?" Jay asked as he finished his chocolate pudding, then placed the plastic cup on the tray. "I mean, we hadn't seen each other in almost five years, and then it was just for a day." Jay seemed to be struggling to find the words he wanted, and Donald fidgeted slightly in the chair. "I want to get to know you again. The other night felt just like I remembered, but things aren't just what we remember. You told me that we've changed, and we have. Both of us have lived almost a decade without seeing each other but a few times. But more than anything, I want to get to know you again."

"I want that too. It's kind of funny, but I've dated guys over the years, and some of them were really nice, but I compared all of them to you, and that wasn't fair to myself or to them. I knew it wasn't likely that I'd ever see you again, but I realize now that I was still hoping to see you and that I was looking for you around every corner." Donald squeezed Jay's hand. "The truth is that I gave away my heart to a boy I met when I was sixteen years old, and I never got it back." Donald stood up and moved closer to the bed. "I think it's especially hard when you meet your soul mate, the person you're truly meant to be with, when you're sixteen years old."

"Tell me about it," Jay told him. "I thought I was going to die when my father ripped me away from you. For the longest time I was angry with him, and then mad at myself because I didn't fight him then and I always wished I had."

"You couldn't, not then. You could later, but not when you were seventeen. But that's water under the bridge now. I'm here, and you're a captive audience," Donald said with a grin. "So have they said how long you'll be here?"

"A few more days. They want to run some tests on my head and make sure my leg is healing properly. The doctors could not believe that my memory has come back, and they're afraid it may have been too fast, but I feel good, so hopefully it won't be long." Jay seemed content to let Donald hold his hand.

"Do you expect to stay in town?" Donald asked. They hadn't talked about much, and it would be his luck to find Jay again only to have him go back to Chicago or somewhere else.

Jay grinned at him. "Dr. Rivers rarely accepts interns, and when I'm finished with my internship, he's asked me to stay on in his practice. He's the best there is, and he has said he's been looking for someone he felt he could take on to expand the practice. Do you think you could be in a relationship with a doctor? It's not easy."

Donald chuckled, moving the chair close to Jay's bed. "When has anything between the two of us been easy?"

"When we're together, things between us have always been easy. Since we were teenagers, the hard part has been being in the same place, and it looks like we may have that problem licked." Jay shifted on the bed before tugging Donald closer. "I love you," he said, and Donald might have murmured something similar in return—he wasn't sure and didn't remember as Jay tugged him in for a deep kiss that made Donald completely forget where they were. "I'm going to need someone to help take care of me for a little bit once I get out of here. My mother said she'd come stay with me for a while if I wanted."

"You could stay with me for a few days," Donald offered, knowing full well that was exactly what Jay was hoping for. "Is there anything special you're going to need?"

"I expect the main thing is mobility, and we'd need to watch out for headaches and stuff like that. After a concussion, there can be effects that take time to come forward, but I've actually felt pretty good for a while, now that my memory's back."

Donald kissed Jay again, this time with heat and energy. "Did anyone ever tell you that you talk too much? Because there are much better things you can do with your mouth." Donald proceeded to show Jay as many of them as he could without doing things that were sure to get him kicked out of the hospital. "I'll shift some things in my room so you can stay there. It'll be nice to have company." What Donald didn't say was that he hoped Jay would get comfortable enough there that he wouldn't want to leave. But he didn't want to say anything or get his hopes up. Having Jay back in his life, no matter how slow or fast they moved, was just fine.

"What is it you aren't telling me?" Jay asked, their eyes meeting seriously. "I can tell because I'm so happy to be spending time with you, and you seem distant all of a sudden."

"It's not you. It's that I'm scheduled for chemo in less than a week, and how can I take care of you when I'll barely be able to get out of bed for two days?" Donald explained.

"Hey—how about we take care of each other? I know going through those treatments is hard, and it'll be good to have someone there with you. So how about we agree to be there for each other, just like we always were when we were kids. Remember?" Donald felt Jay's warm hand slide around the back of his neck, the touch comforting. "We were always there for each other."

"I remember you always being there for me," Donald said, swallowing hard.

"Well, then, let me be there for you now. We need each other. Besides, I seem to remember promising to help you shave your head when the time came, and I always keep my promises." Jay stroked his skin lightly, smiling at him from the bed. "Or at least I try to." Jay yawned, and Donald chuckled. He settled back on the bed, and Donald pushed the supper tray away and sat back in the chair to let Jay doze off.

Sheila came in while Jay was napping, and she sat in the other chair. "He seems to be doing much better," Donald commented in a whisper, and she nodded slowly.

"I think you're good for him," she said, sounding a little nervous. "I can't say as I understand the two of you together... you know, like that, but Jay hasn't been happy in a long time, and he seems happy when you're around." She shifted in her chair, and Donald felt Jay squeeze his hand, letting him know that he was playing possum. "All those things you talked about earlier that helped him remember, I never knew about any of it. Was I that bad a mother?"

Donald didn't know how to answer, but thankfully Jay shifted on the bed, opening his eyes and looking up at her. "No. I won't lie, though; there were times when you were an absent mother."

"Did that make you gay?" Sheila asked, and Donald could see the nervousness in her eyes as if she had already found herself guilty.

"Nothing turned me gay. It's just part of who I am," Jay said, yawning again.

"We should let him rest," Donald said before standing up. "I'll be by to see you tomorrow after work." Donald leaned over the bed and kissed Jay goodbye. It seemed funny, but Donald wondered as he did if he would ever stop expecting each kiss to be the last one. In the past, he'd always been caught by surprise, and now he treated each one like that could be it. "Night, Jay. Sleep well, and I'll see you tomorrow," Donald said before pausing at the door to take one more look before heading home. He understood why he felt this way, and he hoped nothing else would come between them.

DAY 7

EARLY SUMMER
CHINCOTEAGUE ISLAND, VA

DONALD dozed in the passenger seat as they drove. He did that a lot lately, but he was feeling better each day. The chemotherapy had taken longer than he or the doctor had expected. But it was over now, and his hair had even begun to grow back, although Donald had threatened more than once to go bald permanently. Bobbi thought he looked good bald and had voted for that, but Donald decided to let it grow in, and now his hair was getting long enough that he might have to start combing it… well, in a few weeks, anyway.

"Are you all right?" Jay asked as he drove, and Donald rolled his head on the seat to look at him.

"Just a little tired," Donald answered with a contented smile. "I'll be fine. My oncologist said this was normal and that I should rest when I feel tired. And since you're driving, I thought I'd take advantage." Donald placed his hand on Jay's thigh, squeezing a little as they rode.

His cancer seemed to be gone, but he'd had a bit of a scare a few months ago when another bump had appeared under his skin. He'd had it checked, and the lump turned out to be an uneven fat deposit. Donald had lost weight, and the doctors had told him that the body didn't always use stored fat evenly. Sure enough, a few weeks later, the lump had faded away. He was still hypersensitive to anything unusual on his body, but so far everything had been good. There hadn't been any signs of cancer in his last tests, and for that Donald was grateful. He knew only time would tell if it would come back, but both Dr. Rivers and the newly minted Dr. Greene, who happened to be driving at that particular moment, thought that Donald had an excellent chance of remaining cancer-free. They'd already set up regular checkups with Dr. Rivers, and Donald had started a regular exercise program to help keep himself healthy and strong.

"We're about to go over the bridge," Jay told him, and Donald opened his eyes. It had been a long time since he'd traveled this route, at least six years, if he remembered right, when he'd come home for his mother's funeral. He sat quietly and looked out on the huge expanse of water as they crossed the bridge before descending into the tunnel in the middle of the entrance to the bay.

"You love this, don't you?" Jay asked, and Donald gave him a smile.

"What's not to love? Bridge, tunnel, and then bridge again—it's pretty cool." Donald shifted in his seat as they exited the tunnel and began crossing the last bridge expanse before arriving on the peninsula that was Donald's childhood home. "Are you hungry? We left really early this morning, and you only had a cup of coffee."

"I'm fine," Jay answered. "But if you need to stop we can."

"I'm good too," Donald told Jay, and they continued driving. Donald was too excited and nervous to be hungry. He hadn't been back to the island since his mother's funeral. He wasn't quite sure how he was going to feel once they crossed the flats and then the bridge to arrive on the island. "So do you intend to give me a hint as to what this surprise is? You've been pretty evasive for weeks, and that's so unlike you." Jay glanced over for a few seconds before shaking his head. "What?"

"Nothing," Jay said. "I've just been thinking how things work out sometimes. When we were kids, Krepke was the town bully, and years later I met him at a conference and we talked. Up until then I'd always pictured him as the bully I remembered. But he'd changed, and if you remember, he was the one who told me about your mother."

Donald narrowed his eyes. He knew all that, and he'd long ago forgiven Harmon for tormenting him. "What's your point? And what does this have to do with this surprise trip back to Chincoteague?"

"Harmon and his partner have moved back to the island for the summer, and they've adopted a son. He got in touch with me a few weeks ago, and I thought it would be nice to visit."

"Is that the surprise?" Donald wasn't sure what was going on.

"No," Jay answered with a suppressed smile.

"You didn't adopt a kid, did you?" Donald knew he was being ridiculous, but seeing Jay nearly do a spit-take while driving was more than worth it.

"No, I didn't adopt a child, although I am well aware that you'd like one." Jay reached over and squeezed Donald's leg. "I'd like to adopt one too, but in a few years. I just thought you deserved a chance to get away, and you haven't visited in a long time, so I thought you'd like to come home for a while," Jay told him.

Though Donald knew something was up, he let it slide. If Jay wanted to be mysterious, he'd let him. After all, Jay had gone to a great deal of trouble to arrange for this trip and to get the time away from the office. They drove on, and Donald watched the once familiar scenery pass outside the car. A lot of things had changed. There were convenience stores where there had been nothing but empty fields and swamp before, and some businesses he remembered were gone, the buildings now covered with plants as nature did her best to reclaim them. Turning off the highway, they headed toward the island, passing landmarks that had been there since Donald was a child. It was good to see that they were still there, including the roller rink he'd visited most Saturday nights when he'd been in junior high.

Donald craned his head as they passed the NASA facility, with its tracking antennas and dishes that stretched over an open space miles across. "I remember the time my mother took me here for a visit, and a few times we came here on school trips. It was always fun."

"I really should have asked, but have you been back here since your mother's funeral?" Jay sounded concerned, and Donald squeezed his leg to reassure him.

"No. After Mom died there wasn't really a reason to come back," Donald answered, and he smiled to reassure Jay. "I'm looking forward to seeing what the island looks like now. I bet a lot of things have changed, and a lot of things haven't." Donald chuckled as they turned the corner and began crossing the tidal flats. Old billboards stuck out of the mud alongside the road, and he saw egrets and herons feeding in the shallows, just like always. Ahead he could see the bridge to the island, and as they crossed it, he remembered when he'd scattered his mother's ashes.

"What is it?" Jay asked when he heard him sigh, and Donald shook his head as he continued watching. He couldn't quite put into words what he was thinking about, and if he did, it would sound dumb. But he was sort of wondering if his mom and dad had found each other again. He liked to think they had.

The tires stopped rumbling as they left the bridge and reached the pavement once again, turning toward town. The business district looked much the same. Some stores had changed hands, but stores that had been there forever, like The Purple Pony, were still open, displaying T-shirts and hats in the windows. "Where are we staying?" Donald asked, and Jay simply smiled, but didn't answer, as they continued driving. They turned down the main tourist street and drove past Mr. Whippy. "We have to go there," Donald said with a smile.

"Of course," Jay answered. "We can go anywhere you want."

To Donald's surprise, most things looked the same. Buildings had been painted and updated, but most places looked remarkably like they always had, as if the island were caught in a bit of a time warp. Maybe it was, and that was what gave the place its charm. To his surprise, Jay pulled into the parking lot of Pirate Cove Adventure Golf, and he motioned toward the ticket booth. A young man sat inside with the same type of pirate hat that Krepke had worn when Donald had clocked him a good one all those years ago. Jay got out, and Donald followed suit, wondering just what was going on. "Would you like to play?" the teenager asked as they approached the booth. "We have three different courses with varying degrees of difficulty."

"Actually, I'm Jason Greene, and I'm here to see your dad," Jay said.

"He'll be right back," the teenager said, and Jay stepped to the side so other customers could approach. It wasn't long before Donald saw a man approach, and he realized it was Harmon. He'd aged pretty well, and had a smile on his face that seemed genuine and, to Donald's surprise, warm.

"Jay, how are you?" Harmon said rather effusively, with a smile to match, shaking Jay's hand vigorously.

"You remember Donny Pottier?" Jay asked, and Harmon's smile transferred to him without dimming one bit. Harmon shook his hand, and Donald couldn't help wondering if this was the same person he'd known all those years ago.

"It's good to see you," Harmon said, looking around. "My partner, Brad, is around here somewhere, and our son Eric is in the booth," Harmon said proudly.

"Is your dad still around?" Donald asked, and Harmon nodded.

"He helps out during part of the summer. He and Mom sold Brad and me the business a few years ago, and they moved to Florida. They spend their summers here, and winter down there. How are you? Jay told me you had cancer but that you were doing really well." It seemed that Jay and Harmon had spent more time talking than Donald realized.

"I am. The chemo's over, and I'm recuperating and trying to get back to normal." Donald subconsciously rubbed the hair on his head. He found he did that just to make sure it was still there.

"Ah, there's Brad," Harmon said as a tall and lanky but handsome man approached them. "Brad, this is Jay and Donny." They shook hands, and Brad immediately broke into a mischievous, shit-eating grin.

"So you're the guy who gave Harmy the scar on his lip," Brad said, and Harmon bumped his hip. "Don't worry about it. From all accounts, including his, he deserved it. I remember when I asked him to tell me how he got it. When he told me, I nearly gave him another one." Brad seemed almost bubbly, and Harmon looked smiley and happy. Brad slipped his arm around Harmon's waist, and Donald thought the two of them looked good together.

"Dad," Eric called from the booth, and Brad hurried over.

"So you have a kid," Donald said with a bit of wonder. If you'd have asked him when they were kids, he would have expected something completely different.

"Eric's great. Brad's sister passed away in a car accident, and she awarded him custody. That was about five years ago, and fatherhood has been more amazing than I could possibly imagine. We took over the business two years ago, and we've added another complete course and updated the older ones. We bought Seaside Golf last year, and we're in the process of updating that one as well." Harmon looked every bit the happy, prosperous businessman. "There's something I always told myself I would do if I ever see you again." Harmon stepped closer, and Donald braced himself for a punch, but he got a hug instead. "I owe you a great deal."

Donald looked over Harmon's shoulder at Jay, who shrugged. "How so?" Donald asked once Harmon released him.

"The day you punched my lights out was the day I began to look at myself differently. I knew you were gay, because I'd seen you, you know, with Jay, and then you cleaned my clock. I think I sort of figured that if you could do that, then being gay didn't make you weak. I didn't think about it at the time, but that was the start of me accepting who I was. I mean, you put up with the kids at school after that and nothing bad happened to you. Most of the kids still liked you because you were still nice and didn't act any different. It's hard to explain, but you were sort of an inspiration in a weird way." Harmon began to laugh, and Donald chuckled. "I also owe you an apology for what I did to you. I know I hurt both of you."

It was in the past, and Donald accepted Harmon's apology as graciously as he could. "Who'd have thought so much could have come out of a punch in the nose?" Donald shook his head because this was starting to feel a little weird, yet still sort of good. "So have you adopted Eric?" He wanted to change the subject to something more comfortable and relevant.

"Yeah. It was a bit of a fight, but we did it," Harmon answered proudly, and he had every right. He and Brad had quite a family, and they seemed to be doing well for themselves. Brad returned, handing Jay something that Donald couldn't see.

"One crisis averted, but I need to get over to Seaside." Brad gave "Harmy" a quick kiss. "Stop by while you're here and you can play a round for old time's sake," Brad called before hurrying to his car.

"I should get back to work too," Harmon said, and with a wave, he headed toward the ticket booth, and then Donald saw him head out onto the course.

"Let's go," Jay said, and they walked back toward the car.

"Who knew?" Donald asked himself, watching Harmon interact with his son.

"He's a nice guy," Jay said. "I wouldn't have thought he could possibly turn out the way he has when we were kids."

"He was gay," Donald commented. "He thought he had to fight everyone to help hide who he was. I was quiet and tried to stay out of everyone's way, sort of disappear. Harmon fought it. But we both came out in the end, and we're both happy. I suppose that's what counts." Donald opened the car door and slid into the passenger seat. "What did Brad give you?"

"The surprise," Jay told him with a grin before starting the car. They pulled back onto the road, and Jay drove down familiar streets, past the house Donald had grown up in. He almost didn't recognize it. It had been painted, and there were flowerbeds in front of the house. It looked like there were children living there, judging by the toys in the yard. Jay pulled over, and Donald got out and stood at the side of the road as he looked at the house. A woman came out and walked toward him.

"Donny, is that you?" She raced toward him, and he realized it was Kirsten. "It's been years," she screamed, and he returned her hug. "I heard you were coming back for a visit, and I'd hoped you'd stop by to see the place." She hugged him again before stepping back.

"You have kids?" Donald commented as he looked around the otherwise neat yard.

"Two boys. They're with their dad this weekend. I left the island, got married, and when it ended, I came back. The house was for sale, and I got enough in the divorce to buy it." She rattled on just like she had when they had worked together at Mr. Whippy. The topics were different, but she was the same girl.

Donald motioned to Jay, and he got out of the car. "Do you remember Jay?"

Kirsten's eyes widened. "The same one?" she asked, and Donald smiled as he nodded.

"We were apart for ten years, but something kept bringing us together." Donald couldn't keep the smile off his face as Jay stood next to him, an arm around his waist.

"I heard you had *cancer*." Kirsten whispered the last word, and Donald smiled and rubbed his head. "To think I was the one that smoked, and you were always so good. Makes you wonder."

"I finished my treatments about a month ago, and I'm doing really well. Jay's an oncologist, and I met him again when I went in for a consultation. We sort of picked things up from there. He and I live in Milwaukee now." Donald still found it hard to talk about what he did for work. He was never really sure how much he could reveal, so he never said much about it except to Jay, and even then he was careful. "What are you doing on the island?"

169

Kirsten grinned. "You'll never believe it, but I'm Mrs. Whippy now. I bought the place a few years ago, so I'm back to dipping ice cream." The two old dippers both laughed, and Jay joined in. It was so nice to see the people Donald had known when he lived here doing well and coming back. He hadn't realized it until he got here, but he'd missed the island. "Do you live together?" Kirsten asked.

"Not yet. At least not officially, though we rarely seem to be apart. We've talked about things but haven't made any final decisions," Jay answered, and Donald felt Jay's arm tighten around his waist. "We spent so much time apart that we're really just getting to know one another again."

"I know you probably need to get going, but stop by for a cone and we can catch up," Kirsten offered before pulling him into another hug. "It's wonderful to see you again."

"Same here," Donald called as they headed back toward the car. "Did you plan this?" Donald asked Jay as they approached the car.

"Only the stop at Harmon's. I just pulled off here so you could see where you lived," Jay told him as they got in the car. "I had no idea Kirsten lived here now." Jay started the car, and they continued driving. Jay went out toward Mr. Winters's place, and Donald watched as they passed it. Donald knew he was gone now and that someone else lived there.

"Where are we going? Are you taking me everywhere we went together when we were kids?" Donald asked as they continued down the road and Jay pulled into the drive of the white beach house Jay's parents had once owned. Jay parked the car and got out, while Donald stared out the window. It wasn't until Jay opened the passenger door that Donald realized they'd arrived. "Is this my surprise?"

"Part of it. Harmon and Brad own it now, and they rent it out by the week. Since it's early in the season, they let me have it for the weekend. I hope it's okay, but I wanted to have a nice place to bring you to."

Donald pulled his bag out of the trunk and followed Jay up the stairs. "Doesn't it feel strange to you to be back after what happened here?" Donald asked as Jay opened the door and went inside. Donald followed and set down the bags. Things looked different. The stark white of the kitchen had been replaced with warm, beachy colors. The floors had been redone as well, and the white walls had been painted a taupe that was warm and much less stark. The place didn't feel the same at all.

"It's just a house," Jay answered as he set down his bags and immediately moved close, taking Donald into his arms, holding him tight before kissing him hard. "This is our love nest for the next two days, and I don't intend think too much about what happened here, or my parents." Jay kicked the door closed, and Donald laughed as he was swept off his feet and half guided, half carried into the bedroom. "Are you still feeling tired?" Jay asked as they bounced onto the bed.

"No," Donald answered, "I'm suddenly very awake, all over."

"I see that," Jay said as his hand rubbed over the bulge in Donald's jeans.

Donald's eyes drifted closed as Jay worked up his shirt, Jay's tongue probing his mouth as Jay deepened the kiss, stopping only long enough to tug his shirt over his head. Then Jay devoured his skin, sliding his tongue up his neck to behind his ears. "I love this body and the way you respond to me," Jay told him as he flicked a nipple with his tongue. "You always taste so good, like the best flavor of ice cream there is."

"Jay!" What started off as a chuckle shifted to a moan as Jay licked his way down Donald's chest. He carded his fingers through Jay's thick, soft hair and then stilled.

Jay looked up, eyes curious. "What is it? I didn't hurt you, did I?"

"No," Donald said as he guided Jay's lips to his. "I just feel so grateful." Donald kissed Jay hard, holding him as he squeezed his eyes closed. "You stuck with me through all that crap, and there are times I can't believe you did that. Do you know how much I love you for it?" There had been weeks when Donald barely had the energy to get out of bed, let alone anything else.

"I told you I loved you and I knew what I was getting into. I love you for you, not for the sex," Jay said with a wink, and Donald smacked him lightly. He wasn't sure if he should be offended or not, but judging by the hard cock pressing against his hip through Jay's jeans, he decided to take it as part of Jay's love. "And if you remember, you helped me get back on my feet, literally. I spent weeks on crutches, and you helped and never complained even when you were going through chemo. No one has ever loved me the way you do." Jay gathered him into his arms and kissed away the words Donald was going to say. "What was that?" Jay asked once he broke the kiss.

Donald wanted to say so much, but what came out was, "Make love to me, Jay."

Donald heard Jay chuckle deeply before nuzzling his neck, worrying that spot that made him shiver. "I intend to, sweetheart," Jay told him in a deep, husky voice. "I intend to love you until you come apart in my arms." A chill of excitement went up his spine as Jay stroked his skin. No one had ever been able to touch him the way Jay could.

Jay stood up, and Donald groaned slightly at the loss of weight and warmth, but he watched as Jay tugged off his shoes before shedding his clothes. Jay then pulled off Donald's shoes then tugging pants and underwear off his legs, tossing them onto the pile. Jay's cock pulsed and bobbed as he prowled closer. Donald had sat up on the bed to get a better look, and Jay moved him back onto the mattress with a deep kiss before straddling him and pressing him into the mattress. Donald loved the feel of Jay's skin against his, the heat, the way Jay's cock slid alongside his. It was like they fit together. "Have you ever thought that the reason we kept finding each other is because we truly belonged together?" Jay whispered into his ear before sucking on it.

Donald nodded and felt Jay's hands slip beneath his body, cupping his butt. Donald gasped when Jay's fingers ghosted over his entrance, with one staying right there, putting just enough pressure on his opening to keep him guessing, but not slipping inside. Donald ground his butt into the mattress, trying like anything to get something to happen, but Jay was the king of keeping him on the edge, always had been, and today wasn't going to be any different. "Jay, don't tease!"

"Not teasing, just loving," Jay murmured softly, and Donald gasped into his next kiss as Jay pressed the tip of his finger into his body. That was what he wanted. Donald grasped Jay around the shoulders, crushing their bodies together, raking his fingers over Jay's back. He would have lifted his legs, but Jay had them pinned, and Donald growled in frustrated agony. "Damn, you're pushy today," Jay told him with heated lust in his voice.

"Pushy gets what pushy wants," Donald gritted out between his teeth as Jay sucked at the base of his neck. He wanted to feel Jay inside him so badly. He'd been tired and worn out for what seemed like forever. Now his energy and vitality were finally beginning to come back, and Donald needed to feel Jay. He knew that Jay loved him, because he showed him in a lot of ways, big and small. From the way he helped him out to the bouquets of

173

flowers that occasionally appeared on his dining room table when Jay had been over.

"Yes, he does," Jay mumbled against his skin before shifting his weight. "Roll over, love."

Donald turned over, his cock sliding deliciously against the bedding, but not for long. Jay's hands took hold of his hips, lifting them up. Butt in the air, head against the mattress, Donald panted and waited. He never knew exactly what Jay was going to do, fingers, tongue, or cock, so he braced for whatever came next, sighing as Jay's tongue probed his hole. "Jay," he said in a drawn-out moan that he knew made him sound totally wanton, but that was how he felt whenever Jay had him in this position.

Jay's tongue went deep, one of his hands cradling one of Donald's cheeks. Donald shook when Jay stroked his other hand up one thigh before cradling his balls. Every touch had Donald's cock throbbing, bobbing up and down. A slow stroke of Jay's hand up his length had Donald's eyes closing as he gave himself completely over to Jay's ministrations and care. "You like this, don't you?"

Donald tried to answer, but it took a few seconds because Jay chose exactly that moment to slide the tip of a finger inside him. "Yes...," Donald whined, but he really didn't care how he sounded. Jay seemed to know what he wanted almost before he knew himself. "You're marking me, aren't you?" Donald asked as he felt the delicious sensation of teeth scraping lightly over his skin, and Jay twisted his finger slightly.

"Always," Jay told him, warm breath scorching his damp skin. "You're mine. I waited a very long time, and I want you to know that every single day—just like I'm yours, sweetheart." Jay pressed his finger deeper, and Donald's eyes crossed and began to water. He wasn't crying, at least he didn't think he was, but he couldn't stop himself. Having Jay with him here, where he grew up, was beginning to overwhelm him just a little. Jay withdrew his finger and Donald tensed, waiting for what was next, hoping Jay would press into him. Instead, he felt Jay nibbling on his skin, his lover's hot tongue probing him, and his lips nibbling and kissing his skin.

"Yes!" Donald cried as Jay lightly stroked along his length. He'd been throbbingly hard for what seemed like forever. Jay bent his cock down, and Donald groaned from deep in his chest as Jay licked a trail from his hole to the tip of his cock and back again, swirling his tongue around his now pulsing hole before sucking down to his balls and then licking his shaft like an ice cream come. When Jay took the head of his cock into his mouth, Donald nearly collapsed forward onto the bed. He had to brace himself on the headboard to keep from falling, his legs were shaking so badly.

Jay kept licking and sucking him until he had Donald teetering on the edge, then everything stopped. Donald was panting like a marathon runner as he waited once again. The bed rocked, and Donald heard footsteps as Jay left the room. He turned his head to see Jay rummaging in his bag. Then he raced back, and the bed shook once again as Donald heard a bottle snick open. Jay probed him with a finger, and Donald held his breath, waiting for Jay.

It wasn't long before Donald felt Jay press at his entrance, then hold still. Donald groaned and vibrated with anticipatory excitement. Jay stoked his hands down Donald's back as he slowly pressed into Donald's body. The burn and stretch were magnificent as Jay filled him. Donald had to stop the urge to jam himself back against Jay. He wanted it all, and he wanted it now. But Jay was all about patience, a virtue Donald was coming to appreciate more and more. Jay continued pressing into him. Deeper and deeper, fuller and fuller, Jay continued the process of joining both their bodies and hearts together.

Through his passionate haze, he felt Jay's hips press to his and Donald took a deep breath, holding still as he felt Jay jump and pulse inside him. He loved the feeling once Jay had just entered him when he didn't move but he could feel Jay's cock moving on its own. That feeling always told Donald just how much he turned Jay on, because that sensation was Jay's body reacting to him and only him. Jay leaned forward, his chest pressing to Donald's back, and he felt Jay's lips on the back of his neck. Then Jay began to move.

The first glorious retreat took Donald's breath away, and when Jay pressed back inside, Donald gasped. He never could figure out which he liked best, out or in, but it really didn't matter. What he really liked most was Jay inside him. Jay's movements slowly picked up pace, and Donald heard Jay start to breathe harder. "More, Jay... please...," Donald gasped between panting breaths, fisting the sheets as Jay picked up the pace.

Donald felt their bodies rocking together and heard skin slapping skin. He desperately wanted to see Jay, but he also didn't want to move or stop what was happening. Jay pegged that spot inside him, and Donald yowled, grabbing a pillow. "Don't"—*thrust*—"stop"—*thrust*—"yourself," Jay said before stilling deep inside him. "I want to hear you. Fuck, I want the neighbors to hear you!" Jay growled as he thrust deep and hard, pegging Donald's gland with body-shaking intensity. "I want the entire world to know how much I love you."

Donald usually tried to keep quiet, but now he let loose, crying out and damned near screaming as Jay rode him into near oblivion. He could barely catch his breath as he tried to keep from collapsing onto the bed in a heap. His cock swayed and bobbed, slapping his stomach, not giving him enough stimulation, but Donald didn't dare stroke himself or he'd end up in a heap on the bed. So instead, he gripped the bedding and held on, letting Jay take him wherever he wanted.

Jay pulled out with a suddenness that left Donald a little stunned. Then he felt arms around his waist as Jay guided him down to the bed with his gentle strength. "I know you want to roll over, and I need to see you too," Jay whispered, and Donald hurried to get into position. As soon as he was, Jay slid back into him with a deep thrust that had Donald's eyes rolling.

Sweat streaked Jay's chest, and his eyes appeared almost glassy. Jay stroked his stomach before splaying his hands on Donald's chest. "You always feel like coming home, like being part of you is where I should be."

"Because it is." Try as he might, Donald couldn't manage bigger words as his mind began to swim. Unable to hold back any longer, Donald began stroking himself as hard and fast as he could. His entire body was already singing with desire, and he wasn't sure how much more he could take. He and Jay had stopped using condoms a while ago, and every time they were together felt like the first time…. Donald's thoughts stopped as his climax built and his mind focused solely on Jay. He tried to keep his eyes open, somehow managing it as his release built and built.

"That's it, love, come for me," Jay encouraged him, and Donald threw his head back, crying out at the top of his lungs as he exploded in ribbons that streaked up his chest. He lingered in a blissful state for quite a while with Jay still deep inside him. Once his lover began to move again, Donald splayed himself out on the bed and rode the wave that was Jay. He didn't have enough energy left to move much, but Jay stroked his skin as his breathing became ragged, and then Jay stilled, and Donald felt Jay throb deep inside him as he was filled with molten heat.

Donald could barely think or move, and when he felt Jay's weight and warmth on top of him, he hugged his lover close and let his eyes close. "I love you so much," Jay said into his ear, and Donald smiled and tightened his grip, too tired and still struggling for breath to talk. "I didn't hurt you, did I?" Jay asked, and Donald swallowed before answering.

"No," he answered, fairly sure that Jay's concern was from his silence. "I'm just fine," Donald added with a smile.

"Did I wear you out?" Jay asked as he shifted off him and onto the bed. "I sort of got carried away and…." Jay's expression of concern and fear was not what he envisioned for "amazingly-mind-blowing-sex" afterglow.

"I'm fine, Jay," Donald said with a smile as he stroked Jay's cheek. "That was totally amazing, and while I may not be up to full steam yet, I'd go through another round of chemo if that was the reward at the end." Donald tugged Jay down and into a kiss that he hoped was hot enough to put Jay's fears aside and melt the paint off the ceiling. Judging by the dazed expression on Jay's face when he was done, he succeeded, even if the ceiling was still intact.

Donald looked around the room they were in and began to laugh. "Isn't this the room that used to be your parents'?"

Jay lifted his head from where it had been resting on Donald's shoulder. "Yeah, what's so funny about that?"

"Please. Your dad would bust a gut if he knew what we'd just done in here," Donald explained. "Especially the part where you had my butt waggling in the air." Donald's laughter died away when he realized Jay wasn't joining him. "I didn't mean to hurt you."

"No. It is a bit ironic," Jay said without breaking a smile. Jay's dad had only spoken to him a few times in the past year, and one of them was to try to get Jay to testify for him at his divorce hearing. Jay had agreed to testify, but he'd made it clear that he intended to be truthful and would answer any questions, including ones about how he'd reacted to the news that his son was gay. Elliot hadn't taken that news well, and he'd called a few other times, both of which ended with Jay hanging up on him. Then the calls stopped, and as far as Donald knew, Jay hadn't heard from him in months.

"No. It was insensitive and I'm sorry," Donald apologized as he moved closer, pulling Jay back down to curl next to him.

"My father is the one who's an insensitive asshole, and anytime you want to laugh about him, or at him, is just fine with me," Jay told him before giving Donald a kiss. "And you're right, he'd pee his homophobic pants if he knew what we'd done." Jay finally chuckled, and Donald remained quiet because he knew that was probably for his benefit. They lay together quietly for a while, and Donald closed his eyes, not ready to move. Then Donald felt Jay getting restless. Jay always seemed to have so much energy.

Getting up, Donald searched for his clothes and set them on the bed, and after a quick trip to the bathroom, he returned to the bedroom as Jay was bending over to pick up his pants. "Now that's a great view," Donald commented, and Jay straightened up. Don moved into his arms. "Is the only reason you rented this place because it was available?"

"No," Jay answered simply but didn't elaborate. Jay began dressing, and Donald wondered if something was wrong. Silently he kept returning to the crack about Jay's dad and wished he'd kept his big mouth shut. Donald pulled on his clothes before grabbing the bags and carrying them into the master bedroom. Jay had wandered off, and Donald found him in what had once been his room. "I remember the last night I spent in here," Jay said without looking away from the window as Donald entered the room. "I looked out this window every chance I could, trying to see if you would be out there."

"I was. I heard you call for me, and then your dad made you close the window," Donald said as he moved closer. "I saw your computer smashed on the ground, and I watched as you loaded the car." Resting his chest against Jay's back, Donald wound his arms around his waist. "I didn't want to get you in more trouble."

Jay turned in his arms. "I know it wasn't your fault. None of it was." Donald hugged Jay close, and he felt Jay's head rest on his shoulder. "Maybe coming here was a bad idea."

"But maybe it wasn't. We aren't seventeen years old anymore, and we have our own lives." Donald touched the back of Jay's head, and he lifted it, allowing their gazes to meet. "We found each other half a country and nearly a decade away from that day. I have no intention of letting you go again for any reason. So you just remember that if we ever get separated again, I expect you to move heaven and earth to find your way back to me, and I'll do the same."

"Won't happen, because I'm not letting you out of my sight," Jay said with a smile. "I have something for you, and it's the reason I wanted to come here." Jay stepped out of his arms. "I'll be right back."

Donald watched as Jay hurried away, and he heard Jay unzip his bag, and then footsteps echoed through the quiet house as he rushed back, but they stopped in the living room. Curious, Donald walked out in the large room with its high ceilings. "Jay?"

"Do you remember this room? This is where we played video games that first day we met. There was the big-screen projection television right over there, and we stood in front of it as we played. Remember?"

"Yes," Donald answered with a small sigh. Closing his eyes, he could almost remember what the room looked like, but more importantly, he could clearly remember what sixteen-year-old Jason looked like, all excited smiles and a body definitely turning from boy to man, with a narrow waist and wide shoulders. He could remember the laughter as they played, and he could remember the look in Jay's eyes as he turned to him. As long as he lived he'd remember…. "This is where we shared out first kiss," Donald said, opening his eyes.

Jay stood in front of him, grinning to beat the band, holding a small box. "It is. This was where we had our first kiss, and where I wanted to give you this." Jay handed him the box, and Donald stared at it. He knew what was inside just by the size of the box. "I've wanted to give this to you for a while now, but I really wanted to do it here." Jay motioned all around. "This is where I met you, where I kissed you for the first time, and where we declared our love for each other all those years ago. And that never left my heart—even after a decade, I could still feel it. So I had to bring you back here to the island before I could give you this symbol of how I feel about you." Jay stopped talking and stared at him. Donald felt stunned, and he blinked a few times before slowly opening the box. He was expecting a gold band of some kind, but what he saw was… spectacular.

"Jay?" Donald asked as he looked up from the ring to his lover and then back to the box. "Where did you get this?"

"Do you like it?" Jay asked, and Donald nodded. He didn't know what to say. It was a simple gold man's setting with three large rubies forming a stripe down the middle. "It was my grandfather's. He left it to me, and it's been in a safe-deposit box for years. I had it sized for you," Jay told him, and Donald watched as Jay lifted it out of the box, then went down on one knee. Donald gasped. "I didn't want to get you a girlie engagement ring, but when a man asks someone to marry him, he presents the person he loves with a ring. These aren't diamonds, but rubies, because the red is the color of love, and I love you, Donald Pottier, with all my heart, unconditionally and forever." Jay took Donald's hand and slid the ring on his finger. Donald could barely breathe as he watched the ring go on.

"I don't have anything for you," Donald said softly.

"You agreeing to be my partner and husband for the rest of our lives is all I'll ever need."

Donald blinked at Jay, who stayed where he was, obviously waiting for an answer. "God, yes, Jay, forever and ever." Donald's heart pounded as Jay stood up and Donald was tugged into his arms. "I'm never going to let you go, Jay."

"Good. We've said goodbye too many times in our lives, and I never want to do it again," Jay whispered before kissing him sweetly. They stood looking out the windows for a long time, until Donald heard Jay's stomach rumble. "How about heading into town for lunch?"

"Wonderful, and on our way back we can stop by Meatland for bait, and I'll make crab cakes for dinner," Donald offered with a grin.

"How about we buy the crabs and spend the rest of the day in bed?" Jay asked with a mischievous smirk. "We need to celebrate." Jay tugged him into a kiss that hinted at what was to come. "Aw, hell, food can wait!" Jay told him, and Donald laughed before Jay's lips reached that special spot. Yeah, food could definitely wait.

ANDREW GREY grew up in western Michigan with a father who loved to tell stories and a mother who loved to read them. Since then he has lived throughout the country and traveled throughout the world. He has a master's degree from the University of Wisconsin-Milwaukee and works in information systems for a large corporation. Andrew's hobbies include collecting antiques, gardening, and leaving his dirty dishes anywhere but in the sink (particularly when writing). He considers himself blessed with an accepting family, fantastic friends, and the world's most supportive and loving partner. Andrew currently lives in beautiful historic Carlisle, Pennsylvania.

Visit Andrew's website at http://www.andrewgreybooks.com and blog at http://andrewgreybooks.livejournal.com/. E-mail him at andrewgrey@comcast.net.

The RANGE stories

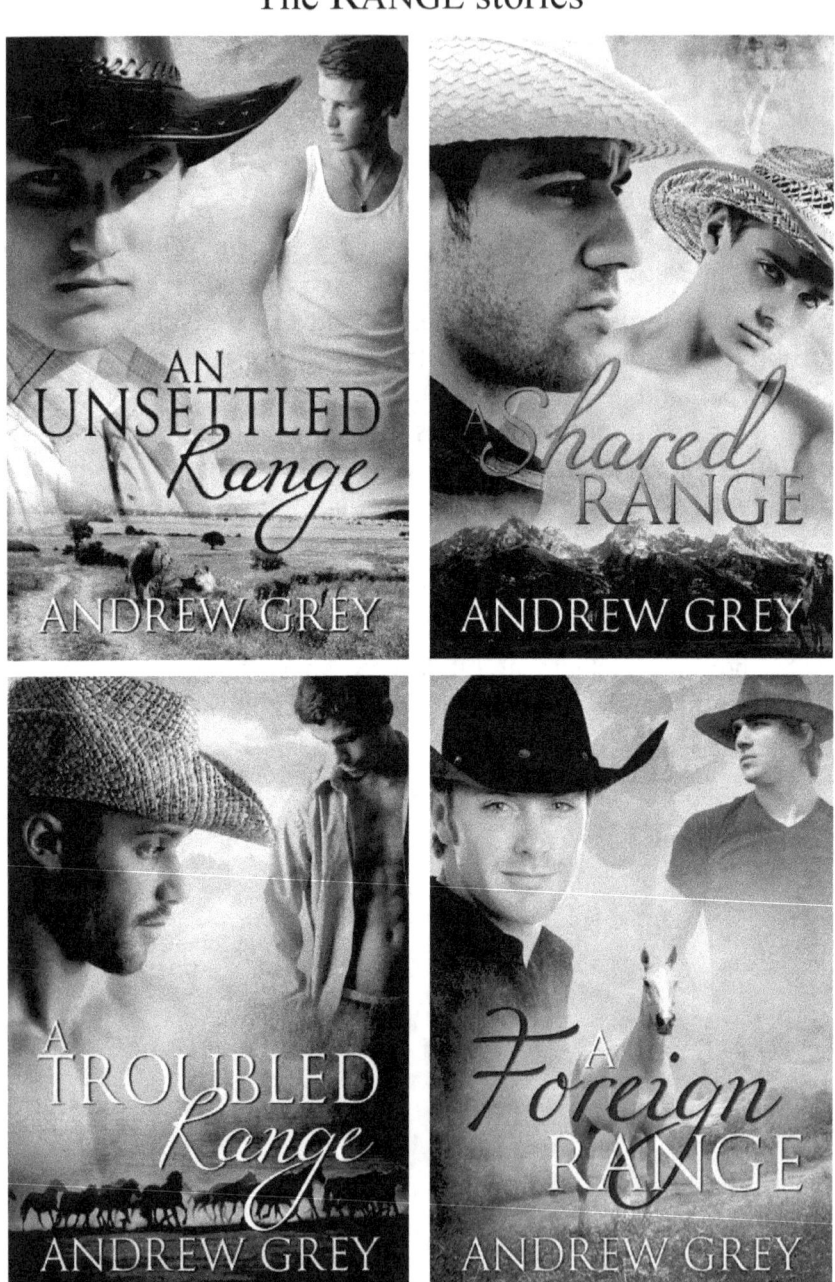

http://www.dreamspinnerpress.com

The ART stories

http://www.dreamspinnerpress.com

Now in Spanish, French, and Italian

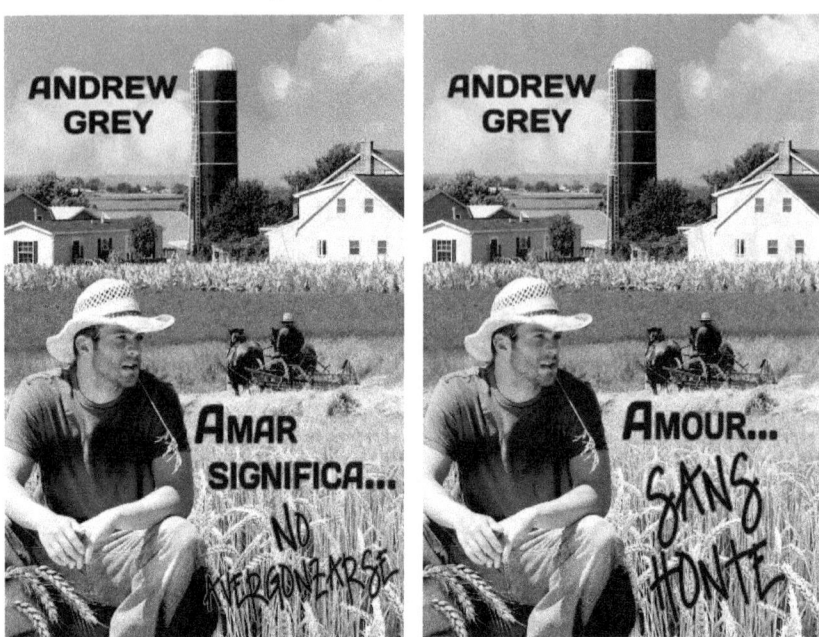

Also by ANDREW GREY

http://www.dreamspinnerpress.com

The LOVE MEANS... stories

http://www.dreamspinnerpress.com

Contemporary Fantasy by ANDREW GREY

Also from ANDREW GREY

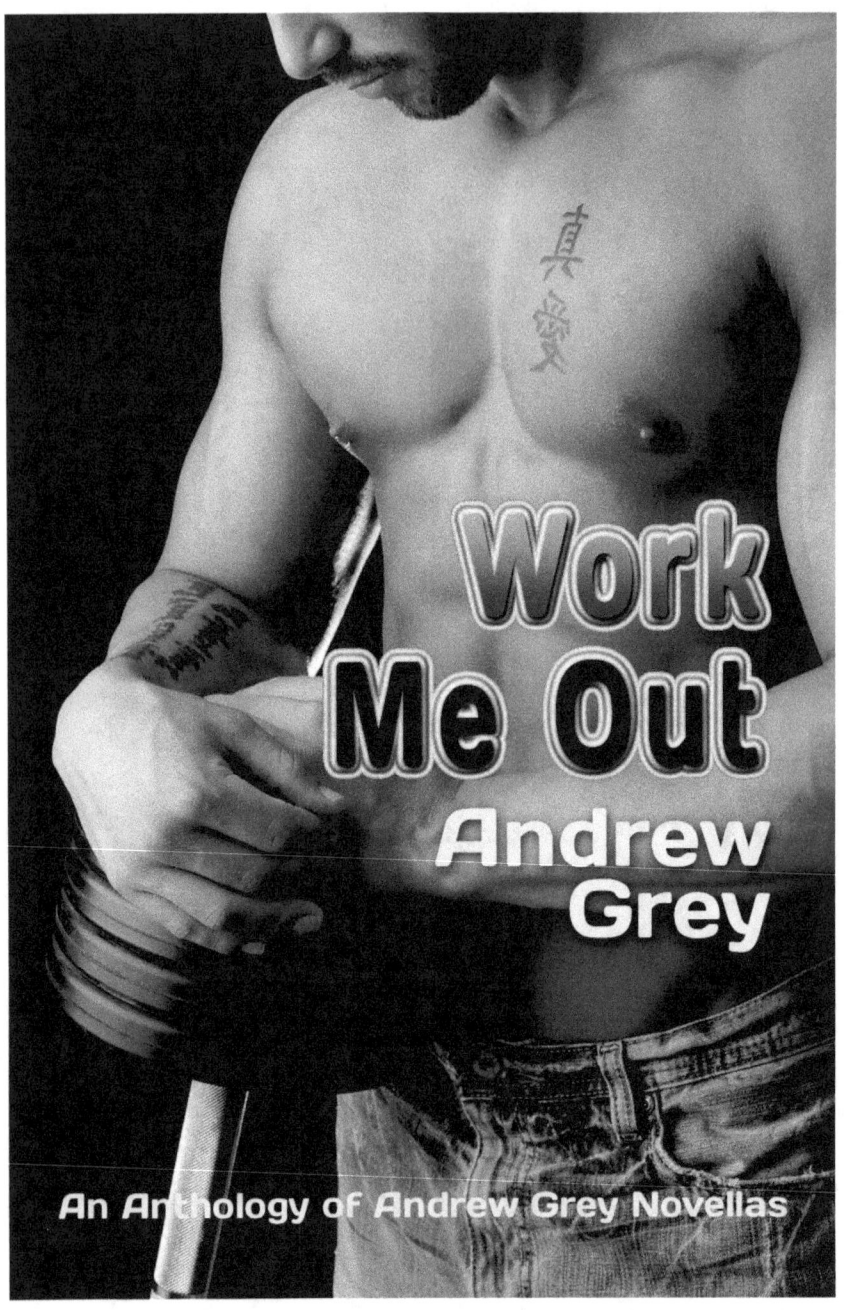

http://www.dreamspinnerpress.com